It's Time

It's
Time
For Action

Robert Mattia

PALMETTO
P U B L I S H I N G
Charleston, SC
www.PalmettoPublishing.com

Paperback ISBN: 979-8-8229-4351-3
eBook ISBN: 979-8-8229-4352-0

Table of Contents

Prologue

I have not been feeling well and instinctively know that something is wrong. I have been assessed and analyzed and have sought several opinions, but I still do not have a definitive answer that would explain my malaise. The doctors cannot agree on a diagnosis. Some results come back as inconclusive and more testing and referrals follow. Others come back declaring me a specimen of good health and the doctors revert to questioning my mental health in the absence of a concrete medical diagnosis. This is when the physician very delicately suggests that a psychological intervention could be helpful.

Even though I know something is physically wrong, I continue with my everyday life. Could this simply be the aging process? Are all those years of uncontrolled behavior, taking risks, filling up on junk food and taking part in questionable activity finally taking a toll? I am screaming but no one seems to hear me. No one seems to sense the impending gloom that I feel.

In my younger years I did not worry about my health. I felt strong and invincible. Now my youthful reckless behavior has been replaced with a health-conscious lifestyle, but I am not sure if it is enough to have a profound effect on my wellbeing. I have continued the physical activities that I thought were beneficial to my health into my mature years, but I am not sure that it is making a difference. My health concerns have evolved into unspoken anxiety. How long will I be able to sustain without making some drastic, difficult, necessary choices?

Then one day it finally happens. I can no longer cope. In addition to intensifying pain, I am now suffering hot and cold sweats. My breathing is labored, I am running a fever, my skin is changing color and is warm to the touch. My emotions are getting the better of me, and I find myself becoming irritable and lashing out in anger. My friends and family can only speculate as to what is going on with me. Some are certain I am genuinely sick while others tell me I worry too much. So, instead of dealing with my poor physical and mental health, I convince myself there is no need to be concerned and continue to party and indulge myself. If this is how it ends for me, I may as well go out enjoying myself.

Meanwhile, I continue to seek better medical advice. There is finally an answer and the results are not pretty. I am seriously ill and I am told that if I do not get prompt attention, I will suffer a catastrophic medical decline and eventually die. At first, I am skeptical and then go into full-blown denial. I am not willing to accept the prognosis. There is a short timeline to get myself back into better physical health. All those years of toxic intake and behavior have finally taken a toll on me. I am told it is a reversable condition, but it will take sacrifice and dedication, and I need to act fast.

Now imagine that this is Mother Earth talking. Our planet is a living breathing body that needs all of its parts to function properly just like we need all of our body parts to function for our health and wellbeing. Our planet needs to be treated with care and respect. We need to repair, replace, and rejuvenate the parts that are in distress. We need to make difficult choices that require sacrifice and take extreme, difficult action if we want to keep our planet healthy for ourselves and our children.

Earth is our naturally furnished home. Our planet is a tiny blue speck in a vast universe. We were given this gift to share with a plethora of plants and animals and we are the only ones that can take care of it. For hundreds of years, we have not been kind to Mother Earth. We did not start taking the care of our planet seriously until the 1970s when Senator Gaylord Nelson created Earth Day. Since then, there has been a great deal of debate about whether or not Earth's inhabitants have an impact on the planet's well-being. To put this in context, have a look around your dwelling. Would you fill it with garbage or run carbon emitting equipment within its walls and then tell yourself it is not causing you, your family, or your beloved pets any harm? Would you leave plastic containers and wrappers stuffed under the couch? You would take measures to purge your home of the garbage and pollutants that could make you seriously ill.

Today, after many years of study, denial, uncertainty, and partisan politics it has been confirmed that we are having a negative impact on our planet. Many people are still unconvinced or in denial. They either do not care or choose not to think about it as they try to squeeze that last gallon of gas into their vehicles. We are all guilty of abusing the planet, not just the big industries. Our portfolios and pension plans are loaded with industries that pollute or that finance the polluters. We want those investment gains and dividends to keep coming. We are torn between good and bad, between wanting a clean environment for ourselves and our children and wanting a secure financial plan. We turn a blind eye, because typically, the ones who suffer the most are the ones who have the least. If it does not have a direct impact on us, there is no need to be concerned.

How did we get here?

Hundreds even thousands of years ago an economic transfer occurred that converted the barter or trade economy into a currency-based system. It started as a slow transition, converting non-renewable resources into currency. Over the centuries, money and currency became the alternative to physical trade. As it quickly caught on, it contributed to the depletion of our resources.

Barter was a natural limit to resource exploitation and environmental impact. Populations were primarily concerned with feeding and sheltering themselves as they worked with what nature had to offer. Accumulation was out of reach except by the few wealthy aristocrats and autocrats who pursued resources by launching armies that marched off to war. Eventually that changed.

The transformation to currency had significantly accelerated by the time the Industrial Revolution caught on in Britain and spread throughout the world. It brought many improvements and innovations to mankind and allowed us to live better and healthier lives. It also encouraged the excessive accumulation of money via the exploitation of resources, commonly referred to as greed. Unlike barter, currency converted the original resource through processing and producing by-products which became harmful to humans. In essence we have produced more man-made products from depleted resources than nature could ever supply. It is a one-way flow.

The benefit of currency over barter is that it converts vast amounts of bulky, natural resources into a compact storage and exchange unit. Unfortunately, that currency can be destroyed or lost at a much higher rate than the original resource that it represents. Currency has a shelf life. The necessary reproduction of currency helps to accumulate considerable monetary gain for the entities that control the resources.

As industry became more efficient so did the exploitation of resources. Environmental damage became more significant. Man-made discoveries exacerbated the problem by adding dangerous chemicals and forever products to our planet. The conversion to currency benefited governments because barter did not lend itself well to taxation. Through money accumulated via taxation, our global governments have contributed fortunes to carbon dioxide producing ventures through major projects, unabated military machinery production and wars. This has all been justified in the name of national security and nation building.

Today, we spend the money that we have created by exploiting and depleting our resources to enter the virtual, computer-generated metaverse. Here we buy fake trees and fake real estate for our utopian make-believe world on remote servers. Servers throughout the world store all that computer generated data eating up massive amounts of electricity. Some estimates say these data centers currently require more than thirty-five power plants worldwide to function and that figure will rise to fifty in the near future. With the advent of crypto-currency, energy consumption has gone into hyper speed. The production of electricity will contribute significantly to global warming if we do not find alternatives to fossil fuels.

Unfortunately, the transfer of resources to monetary units does not reflect what the actual cost of depleting or converting these resources truly amounts to. We have converted these resources to currency at a discount to the full cost. The resource's value has been converted to account primarily for extraction, production, handling, storage, administration, and delivery. There is no cost added for the reduced supply, waste, environmental impact, atmospheric degradation, disposal, or further conversion except via taxation which is not efficiently utilized to combat the existential effects. These costs have been overlooked and ignored in order to bring products to the market as inexpensively as possible. Competition has created a false sense of security that led us to believe there was no end to prosperity.

Throughout the years and depending on the politics of the day, government was the only vehicle that tried to put the brakes on pollution but only if they were forced to by environmental activists. Historically, government has been beholden to two mistresses. One is business and employment; the other is conservation and the environment. In most cases the pursuit of money has won out, giving businesses the advantage to the detriment of the environment. Some legislation has achieved its goals and some has failed. Meanwhile, consumerism has taken a firm root in our society. Many products have become disposable and add to environmental degradation.

The pursuit of currency has led us to destructive practices. For a time, it was acceptable or at least tolerable as we prospered and improved our way of life. Little did we know or care that we were gradually sealing our own fate. The party is near an end.

Join me now on this epic journey to save our planet.

Chapter I
WORK, WORK, WORK

Memory is a tricky thing. It is funny how two people can experience the same event, and at the same time have a different recollection of what happened. I have come to believe that it is perspective that defines recall. This is a story of how a series of unexpected, life altering events changed the trajectory of my life. This is my recollection of how it all began.

The day started as any other Monday morning would begin for this fifty-something-year-old baby boomer. There was nothing to indicate that this would be the day that the shackles of my familiar, well-defined life would be severed and my perception of the world around me and my role in it would forever change. This was the day that started in motion a chain of events that made me realize that not only do the resources of the planet sustain me, but that I have a duty to help sustain the planet.

As I did every morning, I got up at dawn, went for a morning run, shaved, showered, and got myself out the door. My drive to work was a typical Monday commute. I was not preoccupied with what lay ahead in my workweek, rather, I was mourning the end of another two-day reprieve from my nine to five grind. There is something very wrong with how quickly the weekends seem to slip by. Saturdays are spent catching up on chores to free up Sundays for relaxation. Sundays cannot be totally enjoyed because Monday is looming just around the corner. When the cosmos was created, some inherently cruel being must have thought it would be funny to speed up time on weekends. And so, on this day, as always, my musings and my music would quickly pass the commute to the office. Before I knew it, I was pulling off the expressway and into the massive parking lot. As I headed towards the building's entrance, I was once again officially at the starting line of another five-day marathon.

When I entered the office, the first person I saw was Mackenzie, one of my best project managers. She is a tall midwestern woman who grew up on a family farm and labored in the fields of corn with her parents and two younger siblings. There she learned the value of hard work. She has an acute sense of confidence peppered with a down-home appeal and greets everyone she meets with a smile and a solid handshake. She does an outstanding job of planning, screening, organizing, and keeping me well informed of our projects. She first came to my company as a summer student and was eager to do any job thrown her way regardless of how menial it was. Once she graduated with her MBA, I hired her for fulltime employment, and she quickly became my go to person. She is my point of reference, my analytical person, and the person I know who will get the job done. She is always prepared, and nothing overwhelms her. She is a woman on a mission with the charisma, intelligence, and determination to get her there.

I quickly reached my office, and first on my agenda was listening to the many phone messages left by anxious owners wanting to be reassured that their project would be completed on time. Dutifully I returned their calls and did my best to allay their fears. As I did most days, I talked one customer after another off the proverbial ledge. I looked at my watch and realized that a couple of hours had passed, and I was ten minutes late for a crucial meeting. The person that I have kept waiting in the boardroom is Marc, a subcontractor, and the owner of State Mechanical. He built his company single-handedly from a basket of tools and was now one of the state's most successful and reputable mechanical construction companies. Over the years, we have worked together on several projects, and it has always been a positive experience.

I approached the boardroom feeling frenzied but hoping to look calm. My first order of business was to apologize to Marc for my tardiness. He did not seem concerned, and we moved on to kibitz about one another's physiques. Also in the boardroom were Mackenzie, and Marc's project manager Colin. In typical fashion, we took our seats at the large table, with my team on one side and Marc and Colin on the other. I began the meeting by telling Marc we needed more of his help on our hospital project. It was running behind and I explained that I have owners breathing down my neck, concerned that we will not meet the expected deadlines. The statistics they presented me showed that we were in fact behind. Our calculations showed the same results. At this point, I very bluntly told this person that I like and respect that he is not doing enough and that he must step up his game. We needed him to add to his workforce so we could bring the project in on time.

Marc appeared pensive and took a moment before responding.

"Jim, I hear you," Marc replied. "You have been fair with me, but I must tell you we have all those extras still hanging over our heads that have not been approved by the owner. I'm not a charity. I need the money to cover those expenses to keep my business operating. The dollar value of those extras has added up to a significant amount. What can you do to help me?"

Without hesitation or prompting, Mackenzie opened her laptop and searched her files. A spreadsheet filled with data particular to this project appeared on the large television mounted on the wall. She explained that the right-hand column shows the status of each extra that Marc is referring to. At the bottom of the column is the total of the outstanding add-ons which amounted to $55,385.00. She explained that all these extras that have been racked up due to design changes, have been sent to the owner for approval. She then turned to me, and without uttering a word, she let me know that I could take over the meeting.

I turned to Marc and explained, "Look, I cannot approve these extras without the owner's approval. I don't like putting you on the spot, but I am not the villain here. I am the person caught in the middle, tasked with bringing this project in on time. If we don't perform well and on time, it will be that much more difficult to get you paid for these extras. I'll push like hell to get them approved, but you need to work with me and increase your workforce. If we don't get back on schedule, these items will become a contentious issue with the owner."

Marc relented and agreed to my request even though it was putting him in a precarious financial position. After shaking hands, the meeting ended, and we all retreated to our respective workplaces. As I was walking back to my office, I told myself that as far as difficult meetings go, this one went quite well.

The rest of the day was unremarkable, filled with the usual calls, meetings, reviews, and updates that made up a typical day at the office. The only break came around lunchtime. Some of the staff go outside, sit on the patio, and catch a bit of sunshine while eating. For me, lunch usually means quickly devouring a sandwich in front of my computer, catching up on local news and world events.

That day, climate change was the top story. The reporter said the world was heating up and pollution was choking our waterways. He did not tell me anything of which I was not already aware. He reported that scientists say that if we do not clean up our planet by the year 2050, massive flooding and droughts would cause major hardship and death. The scientific predictions were supported with scenes of major flooding in the mid-west and the east coast, devastating hurricanes in the south and horrific forest fires on the west coast. Video of glacial melting filled the screen. After a stressful morning, the images did not help me unwind. Rather, they left me with a sense of helplessness and dread. I was keenly aware that centuries of neglect have slowly destroyed the planet. Was it possible to reverse the damage in mere decades? If not, how would we cope? What would the future hold for our children and grandchildren? All these what ifs were now flooding my mind. It was frightening to think of, but it did take my mind off work. Unfortunately, it was not the relaxing, informative lunch for which I had hoped.

The rest of the day passed in typical fashion and by 6:00 p.m. the early spring sun was setting. I was physically and emotionally drained. My mind needed to be purged of the events of the day, and my stomach needed to be filled. As I walked from my office, I could see that most of the staff had already left. The lights were dimmed, and the cleaning crew were getting themselves organized for their evening cleanup.

As I walked down the hall, I stopped to greet Lori, who had been cleaning our office for years.

Mindlessly, I asked, "How are you doing tonight? Does your daughter like her new job?"

She stopped what she was doing and smiled. She said that her daughter liked her job and that she and her husband were going on vacation the following week. I wished her well and made my way out of the building and headed to my car.

The Carolina air was still cool, and once I fastened my seatbelt, I turned on the heater, set my radio station to easy listening, and I was on the road again. The route leading to my home is leisurely as far as commutes go. The drive takes me down a short stretch of highway to a backroad that winds through the rolling countryside before I turn off onto the lake road that leads to our house. I pulled into the driveway and parked the car in the garage. The thump of the garage door closing on the floor officially put the stress of the day behind me. Another workday had been laid to rest, and the part of my life that I cherish was about to begin.

I walked into the house and yelled my usual, "Wilma I'm home."

My wife Clare poked her head out of the kitchen, blew me a kiss and uttered her customary, "Ciao Bello."

"You're a bit late today," she said. "Was it the Monday crusades again?"

Without skipping a beat, I jokingly replied, "They kept me busy until the wee hours of the morning."

We both laughed at our all too familiar routine, happy to be home and to be with one another. Clare is the antidote to my demanding workdays. She is the first aid for my workplace wounds and the off-framp for my office stress. I never need to tell her how important it is to see her face and hear her voice when I walk in the door. She intuitively knows it. However demanding work can be, it all disappears once I return home to my wife, my best friend.

Clare is a blonde five foot seven-inch-tall Kentucky girl, born and raised in bourbon country close to Mohammad Ali's home. She attended Catholic schools while living in the shadow of an overbearing father that passed on his wisecrack ways to his impressionable young daughter. Rather than buckle to his demanding and controlling ways, she developed strength of character and learned to stand her ground at a youthful age. She was determined to be a better person than her father. She honed her own special brand of humor that was neither hurtful nor cruel that would get her through the challenges in her life. Clare earned her MBA and now works as a compliance executive for a major bank. And of course, she is my partner in life, my partner in crime and my everything.

My life could not have started out more differently. I grew up in a first-generation immigrant Italian home, engulfed in pasta and Mediterranean cuisine in the suburbs of Buffalo New York. Although I was surrounded by loving parents and a large extended family, standing just five feet, ten inches tall, with jet black hair, a protruding nose, and wearing obviously well-worn hand me downs, I had to learn to cope with being different at school. Much of this was done through humor and by being the class clown. It was better to get into trouble with the teacher for disrupting the class, than getting beat up after school for being a timid nerd.

Life was filled with neighborhood pick-up baseball and hockey. Niagara Falls, which is just up the road from Buffalo, was the main attraction in the area and the annual summer road trip for my family.

As a young adult I discovered a passion for sailing and could be found racing on Lake Erie on summer nights and weekends. In my family, higher learning was not an aspiration. Rather, it was an expectation. My education mirrored Clare's, with the exception that her goal was to better herself and break free of her father and Kentucky. For me, it was just something that all good second-generation Italian boys did. I graduated from college with a major in project management. Once I removed that cap and gown, I never looked back. My goal was to become a success in my chosen field, and most importantly, make my parents proud. For the next twenty years I worked on various large industrial projects throughout the United States and Canada, and even did a stint in the Middle East.

Ironically, despite leading a nomadic life, moving from city to city and country to country, Clare and I met at home in Buffalo. At that point, she was ten years into her career, fiercely independent and proud of her achievement in the field of finance. We met, became friends and then we became more than friends. We eventually married, expanded our family with a daughter, watched her grow up, move on to college, and eventually build a life of her own. At that point in our lives, we decided that the cold winters in Buffalo were no longer enticing, and after much research, we decided the Carolinas would suit our needs.

We quickly re-established ourselves in our adopted home state. My daughter and her family soon followed. I started my own project management company and Clare was hired as a compliance officer at a branch of her former bank in Buffalo. Except for the change in geography, our lives were unchanged by the move. We quickly settled into our new home and into the same well-established routine that had worked so well for us for so many years. Despite the grind of the work week, our evenings and weekends together made up for it. Our lives were safe and comfortable, and we liked it like that.

Now that I was in the house, I could smell the distinct aroma of garlic and the scent of sauce simmering on the stove. Once I moved into the kitchen, I had a visual of Clare and kissed her as I do every day when I return home. Even after all these years, I am still amazed that I am married to this woman. She is intelligent, strong yet kind, gorgeous, and most amazingly, she likes me.

Continuing our after-work ritual, I asked how her day was and she shared the highs and lows from start to finish as she did everyday. For Clare, there is never a boring day at work. Every day is an adventure for her, and everything is a story. She can make the tedium and absurdity of a regular workday seem exciting, humorous, and always something worth listening to. With so much regulation in the banking industry, you would think her days would be bland and not worth recounting, but it is never that way with Clare. That is one of the things I love about her. From the day I met her, I knew that with her by my side, our lives would never be dull.

After she finished her work recap, I shared some of my horror stories of the day. Although I approach life with humor, work is something that I can only see through a rose-colored lens once I am long removed from the office. Putting out one fire after another, leaves me little time to interact with others on a personal level. My stories are not as entertaining as Clare's. My recounting of the day is a form of tension relief, and she is the person that is always there to help take the workplace weight off my shoulders.

After changing into comfortable clothes, I returned to the kitchen and poured Clare a glass of Pinot Noir and myself a Michelob Ultra. I started setting the table while she prepared to serve her work of culinary art. We have well synchronized rituals at home that work for both of us. We do not have to say anything, we just know what needs to be done and what is expected of one another. We do this without interacting, and yet we do it as a team.

Over the years we had become firm believers in preparing and eating good clean foods, preferably locally sourced and if possible, organic. We try to keep our carbon footprint as low as possible by minimizing throw away products and containers. It is not a perfect endeavour, but we do our best. Recently, I had been reading books on how our world developed over the millennia, and how the stone age grew to the copper age, and then the bronze age was followed by the iron age.

I found it fascinating to read about how humankind innovated and built our civilization. It is remarkable that it took tens of thousands of years of slow development to reach the Industrial Revolution, and yet it only took us a couple hundred years to advance to where we are now. What drove this rapid expansion of technology fascinated me.

Once dinner was over, I cleaned up the dishes so Claire could take a break. It was only fair. She cooked, so she should not have to do the cleanup too. In the quiet of the kitchen, my thoughts drifted to my childhood and my father. Dad passed away many years ago, but he was still a major presence in our lives. He came to this country as a young man with nothing, but he worked hard and built a life and a family. Despite toiling in a factory all day, he always had time for his children. My father was a photography buff and developed his pictures in the darkroom he built in the basement. Much of our young lives were documented and preserved in his photos and in his old eight-millimeter movies.

Once I finished in the kitchen, I asked Clare if she would like to watch the old home movies with me. I was feeling nostalgic, and it seemed like a nice relaxing way to end the day. As always, she was receptive to my plan, and I went ahead and pulled the projector and the celluloid reels from the closet. We set up an old white sheet as the projection screen, wrapped ourselves in a blanket and settled into the couch for movie night. Watching these old films was like watching vintage movie classics. They were a step back to a time before cell phones and computers when we experienced true reality rather than virtual reality. It was a time when we were less connected electronically, but more connected emotionally. It was a time of innocence that was long gone and that a part of me wished could return.

The first film started with me pedaling my three-wheeler followed by an abrupt scene change to family picnics and gatherings. The films were filled with laughter, happiness, and food, followed by more laughter and more food. The innocence of the world that I grew up in, seemed surreal as we sat and watched. No matter how many times I viewed the reels over the years, the simplicity of the times that I grew up in amazed me. If it was not a kinder and gentler world, my siblings and I were oblivious to the cruelty that existed. The Italian family that surrounded us protected us from whatever evil lurked beyond our family cocoon.

The first reel ended with a familiar flapping sound, and we moved on to a film that my father shot in the 1960s when he travelled back to his hometown in Italy. He memorialized scenes of the farmhouse he grew up in, his family and the fields of olives and figs that he tended to as a young man. He loved filming Italian towns and villages. On that trip, he spent a great deal of time capturing images of Rome, or as he called it, the City of Love. There were videos of the Trevi Fountain, the Ruins, the Colosseum, and the Vatican. He made his way through Old Rome, eventually arriving at the Pantheon, one of the oldest structures in existence. He spent much of his time painstakingly recording its architectural features. He filmed the portico with the large granite Corinthian columns and the circular walls rising to a massive dome with a central opening at the apex.

Entering the Pantheon, he passed through two gigantic bronze doors to an enormous, rounded room. The dome had five rows of twenty-eight sunken rectangular panels and the interior was adorned with twenty-eight columns, square and circular artwork, sculptures, and facades while the marble floor had large square shapes. Back in antiquity twenty-eight was considered a perfect number and held significant religious meaning connected to the cosmos.

As the film panned to the large dome above, I noticed a peculiar feature deep inside one of the panels about three rows up. It was faint and could easily be mistaken for imperfections in the surface or impressions left behind by wooden formwork. I looked at Clare and asked if she noticed it. She had not. I speculated that it could have been the angle of the light beaming through the oculus that revealed the very faint feature. It could easily be overlooked if not for an eye seeking the type of detail that we OCD types are saddled with. As the camera swept around the dome and back to the same position, the mysterious feature had disappeared, no longer visible as the lighting had changed. I reversed the film and replayed the scene. This time I paused the projector. Indeed, there was a feature vaguely visible. It looked like a blurry series of symbols and bars aligned into a pattern.

Trying to contain my excitement, I looked at Clare and asked, "Can you see that?"

"Barely," she responded, not terribly interested in my discovery.

My mind was racing. Had I stumbled upon something that had been missed by centuries of scholars? Why was the symbol not always visible? I reached for my phone and snapped a picture of the still shot. I studied the photo. No matter how I held it, enlarged it, or changed my focus or the view of the picture I could not make out any familiar letter, icon, or symbol. It was at best a fuzzy representation of whatever had been etched in the stone. I could barely contain myself. Had this been overlooked all these years or was I just getting excited about nothing? Do archaeologists already know about this and are they keeping it a secret for some mysterious reason? Claire knew me well, and she knew that I would not be able to let this rest until I could bring it to some sort of logical conclusion. I headed to the home office and fired up the computer. I was officially obsessed. Our evening had taken a major shift from pleasantly viewing home movies of bygone days.

Clare followed me, and we started to research the Pantheon. We learned that Pantheon is a Greek term meaning The Temple of all Gods. It was completed in 126-128 AD, and it was the largest dome at the time. Made entirely of poured concrete, it is still to this day the largest dome made without reinforcing materials. It sits atop an earlier wooden version that burned down twice then rebuilt by the military commander, Marcus Agrippa who was the son in law of the first Roman Emperor Caesar Augustus, originally known as Octavian. Octavian, whose great uncle was the dictator Julius Caesar came into power after Julius was assassinated. A mere teenager at the time, he was named Caesar's heir in his will. By doing so, it vested power to him and allowed him to be named Caesar Augustus. Augustus eventually had his uncle's assassins killed and then also did away with his rivals Marc Anthony and Cleopatra.

We learned that the original Pantheon version had the same name but was built in 25 BCE. After Agrippa's version burned down twice, Hadrian built the current Pantheon but left Agrippa's name on it. We continued to look at various sites filled with pictures and descriptions. We plugged in keywords that we felt could explain our findings, but nothing came up. There seemed to be no records of who designed it, how long it took to build and why it was built. The Pantheon has been a timeless model of architecture even by today's standards. Its design has been the inspiration for many structures throughout the world. Many centuries after its construction, Michelangelo said it was the design of angels and not of man.

While researching I came upon an article dealing with environmental conditions and how it affects the preservation of ancient ruins. I was surprised to learn that even during the Roman era, air pollution was a concern. During those times, fire fuelled cooking, heating, and war efforts. Mining and smelting operations were used for warring purposes and created a cocktail of bad air during this period. So much so, that it created a minor climate change in the Roman Republic and the Roman Empire for about five hundred years. This realization forced scientists and archeologists of the day to dial back their emissions.

This is still happening today as most countries continue mining, smelting, and manufacturing war machinery to the detriment of our environment because we just cannot get along with one another. Much of this war machinery is never actually used in combat, rather it is produced to function as a deterrent. The resources and fossil fuels spent by these operations are immeasurable. One war alone can create more carbon dioxide than a year's worth of civil transportation. War kills, but the carbon dioxide spewed by the war machine is killing the planet.

I continued to read about how climate has a weathering effect on ancient structures made of limestone, which are already susceptible to wear by the forces of wind, water, and sand. Acid rain, caused by sulphur dioxide and nitrogen oxide has accelerated this devastating effect on limestone. Thankfully, through a global effort, acid rain has been reduced via the filtering of combustion and removing lead from combustibles. Our air has improved but we still have one major hurdle to get over. This obstacle to our well-being and the well-being of the planet is greenhouse gases.

My evening of home movies had turned into intrigue. Even though my research had afforded me a wealth of knowledge about Rome, the Pantheon, and the effects of climate change on these ancient structures, it had only piqued my curiosity rather than satisfy it. I felt I had stumbled upon a great mystery, and I had to follow it through to whatever conclusion there might be. History fascinates me, and this was going to eat away at me if I did not find a cogent explanation. But, being a smart man and an attentive husband, I knew I had to put it on pause for now. Clare had already gone to bed, and it was obviously time to shut things down for the night. I began to carefully pack away my father's projector and films. Being his oldest child, I was given the honor of safekeeping one of his most treasured possessions. Our family history was memorialized in that box. It was my responsibility to preserve it for future generations and I did not intend to let him down.

When I laid down in bed next to Clare, sleep evaded me. I was unable to shut my mind down as it was still preoccupied with what I considered the mystery of the Pantheon. I realized that there was just one thing that could be done to ease my mind and put this mystery to rest.

I nudged Clare to awaken her and said, "We need to go to Rome."

She sat up in bed, looked at me and said, "Are you nuts? I'm going to have to restrict your home movie viewing time."

And then, with a big smile on her face she shouted, "Yes! I would love to go to Rome!"

When she asked me when I wanted to leave, I did not have an answer. The trip was just a wild idea, and I really did not expect Clare to respond as enthusiastically as she did.

I lamely said, "Whenever we can find time."

"How about next week? Can you pull that off?" she asked.

I was stunned by her enthusiasm but at the same time I was not surprised. That was one of the things I loved about her. She was spontaneous and always up for a new adventure. It was in that moment that I realized my trip to uncover this mystery was no longer a pipe dream. We were really going to Rome. I told her that I would check my calendar in the morning, and that I should be able to move some meetings around and get away for a week.

And just like that, we were planning an unanticipated trip to Rome. We snuggled into bed and as I was drifting off to sleep my last thoughts were about what we had just seen. I would not be able to rest until this mystery was solved. Some may describe me as obsessive, but Clare says my quest for answers turns me into a famished anteater that digs deeper and deeper until I find what I am looking for. Clare knew that she would not have her husband back until he found a logical answer to this mystery. She knew that we had to go to Rome.

Chapter II
ROMA

The next morning, we awakened to a day of brilliant sunshine reflecting off the lake. The sound of birds calling out to one another seemed to be the only sign of life in the stillness of the morning. We quickly got out of bed and went on our morning run. After a shower and a cup of coffee, we headed out the door and off to our respective workplaces. It seemed like any other day, but I knew that it would not be a routine day. Once I returned home, we were going to book our trip to Rome and put our factfinding mission in motion. On my drive to work, I was oblivious to the beauty of the day. All I could think about was our prospective trip and what we would find there.

Once I was in the office, the first thing I did was let Mackenzie know that I would be away the following week. I did not want to tell her the actual purpose of the trip and how completely impulsive and insane it was, so I told her that I was taking Clare on a long overdue romantic trip to Rome. I elaborated by saying that I could not remember the last time the two of us were able to get away on a vacation. The reason I gave for the short notice was that if we keep planning to take a vacation in the future, it may never happen. One of us would always have something that would tie us down. We decided to be spontaneous and just do it. Although I was babbling, once I finished my official story, I thought it sounded plausible. By Mackenzie's lack of reaction, I knew I had nailed it. Then it occurred to me that maybe she was having trouble trying to digest the deluge of information that I had spewed at her. However, I chose to believe that I was just a very convincing liar.

I assured her that ongoing projects could be put on autopilot for a week. She always had a good handle on things, and I was confident that she could manage. I would be available by phone should there be a dire emergency. Rather than show any sign of panic or apprehension, she just told me to have a wonderful time. She assured me that things would not fall apart in my absence. While I was concerned that I was dumping an unmanageable, unexpected load on her shoulders without much notice, I realized by her reaction that she was excited to have the opportunity to be fully in charge. While I saw my absence as a burden for her, she saw it as an opportunity to hone her skills. If I ever had any concerns about her ability to lead, her confidence put them to rest.

As I navigated my way through another typical crisis riddled day, I was trying to relegate thoughts of our impending trip to the back of my mind. I could not stop thinking about what we might find at the Pantheon. Could it be that I am long overdue for a break from work, and I am seeing something in the ruins that really does not exist as an excuse to get away? Looking at it logically, I feared that the actual answer could be that insanity was setting in. Whatever the case, focussing on workplace issues was difficult, and I was more ready than ever to leave work that day so I could get back to Clare and make reservations for our trip. Maybe once we booked our top-secret excursion, I would be able to settle down and focus.

After a quick dinner, the planning began. We found a non-stop flight that worked for both of us. Next, we started the search for a hotel. After much back and forth, we settled on one that was close to the Pantheon and everything else that was of interest to us. We detailed our Roman trip from flights to rental cars, clicked on send and just like that, all our plans were itemized and paid for. The finalization took a huge weight off my shoulders. It was amazing how the trip fell into place on such short notice. It was no longer something that we dreamed of doing in the future, it was really going to happen. We told one another that we were destined to go to Rome. Perhaps it was some divine power forcing us to do something outside of our comfort zone.

The rest of the week seemed to drag on endlessly. When Friday finally arrived, it felt like a month had passed, rather than just a few days. At 2:00 p.m. we loaded our luggage in the car and headed to the airport for our 6:00 p.m. flight. It was only a forty-five-minute drive from our house, but traffic at this time of day could be a challenge. Once we were on the highway, we could see that it was already backed up and our anxiety levels quickly changed from concern to full blown stress. Our navigation system showed that there was only a ten-minute backup, so we tried to calm ourselves by reassuring one another that we would make it on time. Finally, the seemingly never-ending drive ended. We arrived at the parking garage and quickly found an open space.

As we raced to the terminal, our conversation centered on how long the lines would be, will we have time to sit and collect ourselves before our flight and what will they be serving for dinner? For me, sleep is always challenging on a flight, so I brought a book to read just in case. We deposited our checked bags and headed for the TSA inspection. Thankfully, the line was not too long. We emptied our pockets, placed our carryon bags on the conveyor and made our way through the metal detector. We cleared quickly and headed to the large departure board. Our flight was on time and would be leaving from gate B13. Pending any delays, we would be arriving at the Rome Fiumicino Airport at 8:00 a.m., Italian time.

After the stressful trip to the airport, our boarding went smoothly. We stuffed our carry-on bags into the overhead bins, sat back and tried to relax. The seven-hour flight was uneventful. After consuming some standard airplane cuisine, the lights went out, Clare rested her head on my shoulder, and we drifted off to sleep. We were jolted awake by a blaring announcement that we would soon be landing. I managed to sleep through the flight, and we were awakening to a glorious Italian day. This had to be an omen that we were destined to come on this trip.

Shuffling off the plane, we made our way through customs, retrieved our luggage, and headed to the car rental counter. There I made a feeble attempt to use what little Italian I could muster up mixed with some English words. I realized my effort was futile when the first response from the attendant was a bewildered, amused smile. He then continued to speak in almost perfect English. The agent seemed to be relieved when I gave up my pseudo-Italian attempt. He promptly assigned us a small blue Fiat that he said we would find in stall number fifteen. He wished us a wonderful trip and we were on our way to the parking lot.

After walking for what seemed like miles, we found the car, popped open the back hatch and laboriously stuffed our luggage into the tiny vehicle. We knew that due to outrageous gas prices, our rental would not be the spacious domestically made vehicle we were accustomed to, but this car was ridiculously small. After attempting to familiarize myself with its navigation system, Clare and I decided that for the time being, it may be wise for us to use her phone's maps application to find our hotel. We wanted to be sure that we would arrive at the Corso Suites rather than get lost and wind up at some random destination.

We soon realized that navigating the city would be a challenge. Having a car in Rome meant driving around looking for a spot to park. The roads were lined with stationary vehicles on both sides. After circling the streets for forty-five minutes in congested traffic, successfully maneuvering several roundabouts and winding roads, we reached our hotel. The excitement that had been building since our plane landed, had now turned to fatigue. We checked in, unpacked, and plopped ourselves onto the neatly made bed. After a few moments, Clare was the first to speak. She was both excited to be in Rome and in utter disbelief that what got her there, was an old home movie and a mystery hidden in the film. Regardless, it was something she had always wanted to do. She was now able to strike something off her bucket list and it was giving me the opportunity to pursue a mystery that may have been hidden in the ruins for centuries.

After a brief rest, we decided to clean up, change and do some exploring. There was no time for romance today. We were both eager to begin our adventure. By the time we left the hotel, it was close to noon and hunger and jet lag were overtaking us. Dressed in comfortable walking attire we stepped out onto the sidewalk and planned our next move. Without a destination in mind, we randomly decided to turn right and see where it would take us. The sun was shining bright, and the temperature was above average. Europe had endured some stiflingly hot weather lately and the heat was already causing small beads of sweat to appear on my brow. It was clear that I needed to acclimatize myself to the warmer Rome weather.

As we walked along the street, we passed shops filled with purses, shoes, and clothes. The imposing buildings were ancient, sculpted limestone structures. Row after row of massive block buildings carved with stone images of creatures and long dead Roman figures seemed to stretch upwards to the clouds. Down the street in the distance, we could see the famous white marble memorial Altare della Patria. We continued walking and taking in the sights until the distinct aroma of Italian cuisine filled our senses. We decided that sight seeing would have to wait. Our empty stomachs needed to be tended to. We ducked into a quaint trattoria and were greeted by a personable waiter who ushered us to our table. He started his recitation of the menu in Italian, but he quickly switched to English delivered with a strong Italian accent when he saw the puzzled look on our faces. After a glass of wine, we ravenously devoured a plate of gnocchi with side dishes of artichokes and olives. After a shot of grappa, we were fortified and, on our way, ready to conquer Rome.

Feeling lightheaded and carefree, we were giggling as we made our way down the street. We realized that we were merely two small fish in an ocean of tourists. Everyone was jockeying to take that perfect scenic snapshot. We spent the rest of the afternoon wandering the streets taking in the splendor of ancient Rome. Having a construction background, I could not help but question how all these structures were built. How much time and effort did it take? What tools and equipment did they use? Today we could not even consider creating these colossal buildings. The expense would be unimaginable. We do not have the craftsmen and the economics would not make sense. Except for the artists who carved the marble masterpieces, most of these structures were built using an involuntary labor force. We marvelled at how beautifully the structures had survived over time and how fortunate we were to be able to gaze at their beauty and majesty. I noticed that several buildings were covered in scaffold and a mesh like fabric. We were intrigued as to why, but the answer would have to wait for another day when we were less fatigued. Overall, our first day in Rome was everything that a carefree tourist would expect.

As the cooler evening air set in, we headed back to our hotel room for some relaxation and room service to cap off the night. After an ensuite dinner we decided a romantic evening stroll was in order. This time we walked in the opposite direction. The lights and the atmosphere were magical. We clenched our hands together and aimlessly strolled the quiet streets. Every so often a cyclist, a scooter or a taxi would whizz past us. We met other couples who were also taking advantage of the serene atmosphere. We could hear the clinking of silverware and plates as we passed by restaurants and pizza shops. The sound of Italian conversation could be heard in the street as dinner patrons enjoyed culinary delights while sharing time with their friends and families. It was all so surreal. We were immersed in an unfamiliar environment far from home, and it felt magical.

Once again, we returned to our room. Tomorrow, we would explore The Pantheon. We mapped out our route for the following day, shut our eyes and tried to get some sleep so we would be rested for the big day that lay ahead of us. The restful sleep that we hoped for did not happen. Rather, we endured an endless night of tossing and turning. We were too physically exhausted and mentally exhilarated.

We awoke to the sounds of Rome coming to life. Below our window we could hear car horns and the voices of people making their way to work. For the first few moments that we were awake, we had forgotten what the real purpose of this trip was. After a shower and a cup of coffee we made our way out of our room, slipped into the narrow elevator, and headed for the café. We would need sustenance to take us through the day. As a child, my mother made me very aware of the importance of a good breakfast, and to this day that is a vital part of my daily routine. I thought of how she would tell me that nothing good happens without a good breakfast. We were anxious to get on with our plans and there was no time to wait for a warm breakfast to be prepared. We decided to pick up a scone and fruit at the hotel café instead.

We headed out to the street with our breakfast in hand. The morning buzz of traffic and the flurry of people hurriedly making their way to their destination, created a sense of excitement and vitality in the city. We stepped up our pace as we made our way to the Pantheon. The ten-minute walk was invigorating. We paused and stood in awe once we arrived at the ancient structure. We imagined all the historically famous people who had once walked the same cobble stones that we were walking. Once we entered the building the sheer size of the structure and its significance in history was overwhelming.

I looked at Clare and said, "This is amazing."

She nodded her head in agreement. She was too spellbound to articulate any words.

We were both mesmerized with the magnificence and the grandeur of the structure as we passed through the massive bronze doors to the center of the building. I imagined my father standing there many years ago. Slowly and methodically, I examined each square foot of wall without moving from the spot where I was standing. I then looked skyward to the massive 142-foot diameter dome and the twenty-seven-foot opening at its peak that lets in both sunlight and rain. For a moment I stood captivated by the splendor and sheer detail in the workmanship. The amount of effort it took to create this masterpiece of architecture must have been monumental.

Once I had fully absorbed the magnificence of the building, it was time to focus on our mission. I pulled my phone from my pocket and opened the picture of the Pantheon that I took from my father's home movie. Raising my phone as if to take a picture, I instead tried to match the photo to the specific location on the domed ceiling. I gradually moved the phone up and down and side to side until I came upon the location that matched the photo on my phone. I retraced my movements a second time to ensure accuracy and I was satisfied that I had pinpointed the panel appearing in the picture. I lowered the phone and gazed at the spot. There was no visible sign of the markings, so I reached into my pocket for the small set of binoculars I had packed. As I peered through them, I noticed a very faint anomaly where I thought the markings would be. I could not be sure whether it was just an uneven surface or if it was something more mysterious.

I wandered around until I spotted Clare. She was busy marveling at the sculptures and artifacts. I moved purposefully towards her and asked her to come to the spot where I was standing and look through the binoculars. Once she was in position, she agreed that something appeared to be there but could not verify what it was. The markings were too faint. We wondered how and why this symbol would be captured on film but would not be visible otherwise. We surmised that when my father made his visit here, the lighting at the time must have been exactly right to reveal the markings. It was possible that the etching was nothing more than the signature of the artisan who helped build the Pantheon. In hushed voices, we discussed how we would be able to investigate the marks. If we were to address it through proper channels, we may be seen as a foolish couple seeking fame with some outlandish claim of a historic discovery. We did not want to be accused of sensationalism or be labelled 'that couple' and be remembered in notoriety. We had to regroup and decide how to proceed.

Chapter III
PANTHEON

Our next move came to us quickly and we acted without hesitation. We decided that our minds would work more clearly once we had sustenance. We made our way outside to the tourist filled piazza. Directly across the street from the Pantheon was a collection of tables and chairs with large umbrellas shading the patrons from the noonday heat. The sun was shining bright and hot, beaming down on the square that was alive with the sounds of tourists. We made our way through the crowd and spotted a vacant table and chairs. Patrons were enjoying tiny cups of espresso and biscotti; others were savoring bowls of gelato. We decided that for ourselves the perfect lunchtime food in Italy would be pizza.

"This is perfect," I said. "I love it. Can you believe this Clare?"

"I know. I feel like I have to pinch myself," she replied. "I can't wait to retire so we can do this more often. We'll have to bring our grandson one day."

Within minutes our server was there to take our order of pizza and two glasses of vino. We sat in this large area filled with tourists, and yet we felt like we were in our own little bubble. It was amazing how peaceful we felt sitting in the midst of a bustling crowd. We sat without speaking and soaked up the environment.

"Is this not a great vacation, Clare?" I asked.

She replied, "It sure is. I'm so glad we did it. We needed this."

Our conversation once again shifted to the purpose of the trip. Based on my father's home movie, it was the sunlight beaming through the oculus that revealed the marks. Unfortunately, I did not know what time of day or what month it was filmed. It was then that we developed what now seems like a crazy plan, but at the time made perfect sense. We decided that if sunlight creates the shadows that reveals the otherwise hidden features, then it would make sense that we could use artificial light to re-enact the sun's rays. The only drawback was that we would have to get inside the Pantheon during hours of darkness. If we could do that, we might be able to shine light from various positions into the space and see the markings.

"Clare, tell me honestly if that makes sense to you," I implored.

She replied, "I made a note of the visiting hours when we were there. They open at 8:30 a.m. and close at 7:15 p.m."

It was at that moment where we moved beyond the point of being realistic and ventured into uncharted territory. We decided that somehow, we had to have access to the Pantheon after hours, during the night when no one else was present. We had to figure out how to get into the building after tourist hours. I suggested that if it was a Catholic church, it should be open all hours. Clare shot that idea down. She pointed out that if it was open all day and all night but the signage would not indicate specific times. We proceeded to brainstorm crazy, outlandish, improbable ideas on how to gain access, but every plan that we imagined would have the Carbonari all over us. Here we were in Rome, two middle class grandparents trying to figure out how we can break into a landmark at night. It sounds outlandish now, but somehow in that moment, it did not seem that crazy to us.

I looked across the Piazza to the Pantheon and carefully examined it top to bottom. My guess was that the building was about seventy feet high. I pulled out my phone and opened my maps application to get a bird's eye view of the dome and studied it carefully. I thought I was onto something.

I showed the map to Clare and said, "Outside at the base of the dome is one set of stairs that leads to another that takes you up to the opening at the top of the dome. And look at this. There is a set of stairs that takes you from the roof at the back of the building back to the base of the dome."

She looked at me incredulously and said, "Are you crazy? Do you really think we are going to do something that stupid? Look, we came here, we went to the Pantheon and we found what may or may not be the markings in your father's video. We still have six days left before we have to go home. Why don't we just have that romantic getaway that we hoped for, rather than potentially ending up in an Italian jail?"

I looked at her and uttered words that this law-abiding citizen never thought would come out of his mouth, "How else are we going to get in? The only way we can do it is by breaking in. We have come this far, why can't we keep going until we solve this mystery?"

She immediately countered and said, "Are there not any doors that we can go through like normal human beings?"

"I'm sure there are but the doors will be armed and we cannot be sure where they lead to," I responded.

She looked at me in disbelief and said, "Just how do you realistically think you can pull this off? For a guy that has never even had a parking ticket, you are now talking about scaling and breaking into a building in a foreign country. My mainstream, law abiding husband suddenly sees himself as Spiderman, and quite honestly that is a bit scary. Who are you? We need to let this go."

I could tell by Clare's response that she thought I had lost my mind. Luckily, the waiter's timing was impeccable. It was at this moment that our food arrived. We raised our glasses of wine and toasted without mentioning anything specific. After devouring the delicious pizza and a couple more glasses of wine we paid our bill and headed towards the Pantheon. Our stomachs were full and our confidence was enhanced by the wine. It was at this point that I suggested we case the place. We could walk the perimeter of the building in hopes that a point of entry would catch our attention. I suggested that we stroll to the portico and then slowly walk around the exterior walls carefully eyeing each detail. The wine had subdued Clare's apprehension, and my idea did not seem quite as ridiculous to her after lunch.

As we neared the back of the building the grey concrete gave way to brick and mortar broken up by doorways and windows. It appeared as if this part of the structure was an add-on subsequent to the original build and there was no guarantee that these openings would get us into the rotunda. As we turned the last corner, parked next to the building with yellow tape around it and bright neon orange pylons at each corner was an elevated platform lift sitting idle. A maintenance crew must have left it behind. This caught my attention and got me thinking. That lift must be there to access the roof of this brick portion of the structure. This could be what we were looking for, but we continued our investigation until we had made a complete circle around the building. Since there were Carbonari along the way, we had to appear touristy so as not to be too obvious in our search. Just for show, we stopped every so often to marvel at a feature when we were in eyeshot of the Rome police. At the end of our outside perimeter tour, I felt comfortable with the information we had gathered. We decided to go back inside for a final look, this time to get a feel for the space before going back to our hotel for the day.

Once we finished casing the inside of the building, we stepped out onto the piazza where the beaming afternoon sun drenched us in warmth. Holding hands, we strolled through the stone canyons of ancient buildings filled with tourists and returned to our hotel. Entering the ancient structure with its modernized interior furnishings, we made our way to the elevator and up to our room. Clare moved straight to the large window and tore open the curtains to expose a magnificent view of old Rome. We stood for a moment and soaked it up. I then took a seat at the desk while Clare moved to the bed, removed her shoes, and rubbed her aching feet.

Once we had a chance to collect ourselves, I suggested that we should go back to the Pantheon that night after dark. Clare agreed, seeming to have let go of her apprehension. We started throwing about ideas.

"The lift that was outside could get us onto the roof where we could access the dome by using all those stairs up there. We could bring rope and lower ourselves down into the rotunda," I suggested.

"Are you nuts?" Clare asked. "First of all, I am not going to fall to my death trying to shimmy down a rope. We are not commandos. You are not James Bond or Indiana Jones for that matter. Do you realize that if we survive we'll find ourselves featured on an episode of America's Dumbest Criminals. Jim, you are going too far with this. When we planned this trip, I was thinking we would just sit in that spacious room and watch the sun pass to see if it revealed the markings. The rest of the trip would be for pleasure and romance."

Not deterred, I countered, "I hear you Clare, but we sat in that big space for almost two hours and nothing happened even as the sun was shining through at different angles. The markings need the correct angle of light to appear and maybe a specific time of year too. My father travelled here sometime during the summer. It's only April. We have to get creative or this will be a wasted trip."

We sat in silence and then Clare had a brilliant idea. She suggested that we get a drone with a camera.

"Yes," I said enthusiastically. "Great idea. Now we just need a source of light. We can get one of those high intensity rechargeable flashlights. We use them all the time on the job when we need massive amounts of light. You know what Clare; this is looking more promising all the time. We can do some more reconnaissance tonight and check out the lift one more time."

We continued to formulate our strategy. Now that we were on the same page, the plan seemed to come together much more easily. We decided to pick a night to use the lift to get onto the roof, make our way to the dome, and then take the stairs to the large opening. Once we were in position, Clare would shine the flashlight, and I would operate the drone taking videos and pictures. We decided that if we put our plan into motion late at night, our mission should be accomplished within an hour.

With our plans set, our next course of business was to find an electronics store to buy the drone and flashlight. Our online search indicated that there was one about a twenty-minute drive away. We left our room, squeezed ourselves into our mini-mobile and drove through the winding cavernous roads of Rome. We finally arrived at a small store situated on a narrow street where the buildings' walls were covered with graffiti. This seemed to be quite common in Rome. Entering the shop we went directly to the large display of drones. Unfortunately, everything was written in Italian so I needed to get the clerk's attention.

Hoping he spoke English, I approached him and said, "Excuse me sir, I am looking to buy a drone."

He looked at me and replied in that familiar Italian accented English, "Of course. How do you plan to use it?"

There was not a chance in hell that I was going to tell him what I actually needed it for, so instead, I gave him the specifications. It needed to be able to operate for about thirty minutes and a good zoom camera was necessary. It also needed to be as compact as possible. He showed me various models and explained the features. I decided on a compact black version with four collapsible rotors and a small high-powered camera. Collapsed, the drone almost fit into my open palm. Next, we sought out a high-powered flashlight. We settled on a 50,000 lumens rechargeable rescue style model. With our technology taken care of, we headed to a department store to buy dark clothing and a backpack to transport the equipment. We also picked up a black cap to cover Clare's blond hair. Once we had taken care of our equipment and clothing needs, we headed back to our room. There we laid out all our purchases and started to unpackage and assemble our new toys. We plugged the flashlight and drone battery in and I started reading the instructions.

After about two hours I unplugged the batteries and evaluated the flashlight. Perfect. Next we decided to see what our small but powerful drone was capable of doing. I started it up and the twirling of the rotors gave off a harmonic hum. Slowly and deliberately, I moved the toggle on the remote and raised the drone about a foot off the floor and put it in hold mode. Then I carefully moved it in one direction and then in another. I kept playing with it until I felt comfortable flying it around our room. After about fifteen minutes I brought it down to the floor with a safe and uneventful landing.

With the help of the downloaded app and ten minutes of reading the instructions over and over again, I figured out how to pair the camera with the drone. It should have been simple, but it was not as easy as I thought it would be. I have used Bluetooth effortlessly in the past, but on this day, I could not get it to connect with the drone. Was this an omen trying to steer me away from a crazy plan or was it just too much adrenaline blocking my brain power? My ten-minute battle with the camera ended successfully with my victory over the resistance. I was able to raise the drone to just under the ceiling height and turn on the camera. I could clearly see the upper walls of our hotel room that were adorned with moldings and mini sculptures. The detail was phenomenal as I zoomed in and out. We were literally jumping up and down with excitement.

"This is fantastic, Clare," I said.

She shared my excitement and pointed the flashlight at me as if she was interrogating me, and said, "Well Mr. Bond, we have unraveled your sinister plot and the authorities are on their way to lock you up. You thought you would get away with this didn't you? Not a chance."

We both laughed but deep down we knew that if we got caught we would be in deep trouble. Looking back, it should have deterred us, but it did not.

It was past midnight by the time our equipment was operational, and we headed out to see what goes on after dark in the vicinity of the Pantheon. Dressed in our typical touring attire we left the hotel and walked unassumingly and hopefully inconspicuously toward the Pantheon. The streets were noticeably quiet and it was no different when we reached our destination. There were stragglers mingling about the piazza but mostly it was just people passing through on their way to another destination. The ancient building looked even more gorgeous in the dark of the night with the moonlight bathing it and the surrounding area enshrouded in an angelic white tint. We slowly walked the perimeter of the building. When we arrived at the lift we found it fully extended up to the edge of the roof. We surmised that the night shift must still be at work making roof repairs even though we could find no sign of life.

Turning to Clare, I said, "You wait here and be the lookout."

I moved closer to the lift and noticed the control panel had a key dangling from the toggle switch. Coming from a construction background, I knew that this was a safety measure in case the workers needed to descend but were unable to do so from the upper control unit. A rescuer below would be able to control the lift from the ground. Regardless, I pulled the key off the toggle and searched my pockets for a pen and a piece of paper. I drew an outline of the key on a business card and jotted down the imprinted key manufacturing number. Quickly and quietly, I replaced the key and walked back to Clare's side like nothing had happened. Without saying a word, I showed her the card and she knew exactly what it meant.

We left the Pantheon and strolled the streets, hoping that the construction crew would be gone by the time we returned. We circled three times, but the crew was still at work. Finally, at about 1:30 a.m. the lift was retracted and cordoned off. It looked like the magic time to return with our drone and complete our mission would be after 2:00 a.m. We headed back to our room and were able to finally get a good night's sleep knowing that our reconnaissance trip was successful and we had the tools to execute our mission.

The next morning, we awoke to a knock on the door from housekeeping. I looked at the clock and was surprised to see that it was after 10:00 a.m. Being an up at dawn type of guy, sleeping in this late was unheard of. Unable to drag myself out of bed to tell the very polite worker to come back later, I rudely shouted to her from the bed. Within minutes, we were slowly forcing ourselves out of what felt like an outlandishly comfortable bed, showered, dressed, and headed out to the café for a coffee and pastry. We ate quietly, not wanting anyone to overhear our conversation and report our planned top-secret operation. The beautiful thing about being married to my best friend for so many years was that we could talk without speaking and still know exactly what the other person was saying.

After drinking a couple of cups of coffee and savoring decadently sweet and rich pastry, we were ready to face the day. Our stomachs were full and our minds were once again alert. Leaving the café, we strolled to a cramped knickknacks store full of odd products. I had noticed it the previous day and thought it might be a place that I would like to browse through, but today I looked at it through an entirely different lens. This might be a place that could make us a duplicate key for the lift. Just inside the door, near the cash register, we found a key rack filled with assorted sizes and shapes. Luckily, I was able to find the one that matches the stamping I recorded the previous night. Next, I picked up a triangle shaped file, a box cutting knife and a vial of crazy glue.

An elderly gentleman sat hunched down in his chair behind a cluttered counter. I surmised that he had spent his whole life as the proprietor selling his wares to one tourist after another. He spoke words of Italian that I did not understand, but nonetheless he wrote up a receipt and handed it to me. I understood the amount of the purchase and handed him two five-euro notes and told him to keep the change.

He smiled and said, "Grazie."

We returned to our room where the bed was made up and fresh towels were in the bathroom. The housekeeper did not seem to hold my rude morning reply against me. Clare settled in to read her book and I sat down at the desk with the break and enter tools I purchased at the Italian dollar store. With the knife, I carefully cut out the key shape I copied onto the business card. Then I glued the template to the blank key and waited fifteen minutes instead of the usual one minute for the glue to set solid. I did not want the paper to shift while I was carving the key. Using the file, I started to whittle away the excess metal until I worked my way down to the template. I rubbed the key softly to smooth out the edges. Once my handiwork was complete, I was quite impressed with my ingenuity.

Now it was time to sit down and detail our every move. I stuffed the drone and flashlight into the small backpack followed by two long sleeved black tee shirts and a black cap. We reviewed our plan step by step with intricate detail, from the moment we would leave our room to when we expected to accomplish our goal. We then went over it repeatedly looking for potential flaws in our plan. Even though we felt prepared to execute our mission, we were still apprehensive. The nervous tension was both exciting and scarry at the same time.

With about eight hours to go before starting our operation we decided to take a leisurely walk and visit the tourist sites of Rome. It was a warm day with a slight breeze and sunshine. We decided that the weather was perfect for a stroll to the Colosseum. We made our way through streets filled with structures commissioned by ancient rulers and found our way to the entrance. We could not help but be amazed at the size of this masterpiece of Roman architecture. The Colosseum is the world's largest amphitheater. Scavengers pillaged it during its decline to build other structures throughout Rome such as St. Peter's Basilica. Pope Benedict XIV saved it by declaring it a holy site. Walking through the structure, I imagined gladiators brandishing weapons while defending themselves in a fight to their death. I could hear the cheering crowds and the Emperor giving the thumbs down as exotic animals entered the ring and charged the lone warrior in a fight for survival.

After touring the massive structure, we wandered the grounds stopping to admire the Arch of Constantine. There we met an Italian couple who helped us with directions. They were so amiable that we invited them to join us for a drink. We headed to a quaint nearby venue that they recommended. There we indulged in glasses of Prosecco and compared our lifestyles. Alfredo was a stereotypical version of the Italian man. He dressed impeccably and had a full head of jet-black hair and a strong chin. He could have been one of my relatives. In broken

English, he spoke passionately of how the city draws you in and blesses you with romance. He referred to Rome as the City of Love, just as my father did. When I asked him why so many structures had scaffold and mesh surrounding them, he explained that these were renovations attempting to slow the aging process and preserve the limestone. He said the environment had not been kind to the ruins so it was up to this generation to restore and hopefully slow down the process.

His charming and angelic fiancée told us how Rome was a magical world filled with excitement and mystery. They both grew up, studied, and worked here and yet the city had not ceased to dazzle them. Money, they said was just a vehicle to live a life of discovery and to share the beauties of our earth with family and friends. Rather than have possessions which hold no emotional connections they said they preferred to lavish themselves and their family with experiences and enjoyment. In their eyes, this was the secret of life. It was not about having, rather it was about doing. Naïve or not, it was refreshing to hear their point of view. We explained to them how economics played a significant role in the North American culture and how the quality of life was contingent upon financial achievement. After an exhilarating conversation and more Proseccos, we stood, embraced, and bid one another a warm farewell knowing that we would most likely never meet again, but that this brief encounter had been meaningful.

We walked back to our room and went over the details of our pending undercover mission once more. We unplugged the batteries, checked the nap sack, and read our checklist over and over again to ensure we had not missed anything. After feeling fully prepared for the late night ahead, we decided to catch a quick nap. Clare set the alarm for 1:00 a.m. which would give us much-needed shuteye before our risky adventure would begin. Unfortunately, I could not stop thinking about what lay ahead of us. It was mind boggling that we were here in Rome and we were actually going to break into the Pantheon. What would our family or anyone that had ever known us think? The only logical answer that came to mind was that aliens had invaded our bodies.

Chapter IV
WHAT NOW

When the alarm sounded, I immediately awoke even though I was not sure that I had actually slept. I quickly reached over and slammed the off button on the alarm. I stared at the ceiling thinking about what laid ahead of us once we left the hotel. As determined as I was to carry through with this adventure, I was fully aware of the absurdity of what we were about to do and the risk that was involved. There was no explanation as to why this was so important to me and why I was willing to potentially risk my life and my future to see this through. Regardless, I did not intend to back off until I had an answer one way or another.

I took a deep breath, looked at Clare and asked, "Are you ready for this?"

A small part of me was hoping that her logic and common sense would kick in at this point and bring me back to reality. I expected her to say that we have had our fun but it was time to devote the rest of our stay in Italy to relaxation and enjoying one another's company.

Instead, she said, "Let's do this."

My outlandish plan had captured Clare's imagination and she seemed to be all in. Conflicting emotions of apprehension and excitement coursed through my usually conservative body. I knew that after tonight we would no longer be a stereotypical, respectable, middle-class couple from the United States. This evening we would become stealthy commandos and hopefully, not notorious criminals. This was so out of character for us, but at the same time it made us feel so alive. We had broken free of our nine to five existences. Whoever would have thought a shadow on an old home movie would prompt us to take such a risk.

We jumped out of bed and dressed in our camouflage gear - dark pants, shirts, sneakers, and a dark hat for Clare. I double checked the backpack for at least the thirtieth time to make sure that everything we needed for our mission was inside. The key was still in my pocket. Everything seemed to be in place. We both took a deep breath, high-fived one another, left the room and made it to the ground level via the fire exit. We did not want an elevator camera to capture our images. Once we reached the street, we were struck by how bright the moonlight was. We could almost see clearly, even though it was the dead of the night. The silence on the dimly lit street was eerie. It was as if we were the only living, breathing, human beings in Rome and we were trespassing by being out on the street. Nonetheless, we made our way towards the Pantheon, watching for any movement that would indicate we were not alone, or even worse, that someone was following us.

We reached the Piazza and stopped to survey the open courtyard that was void of human life. Our eyes scoured the buildings and streetlights for security cameras. Except for two cameras, it seemed like all was clear. For such a popular tourist spot, security seemed quite lax. We clasped hands and walked through the courtyard with a playful stride to give the appearance of a romantic couple out for a late-night stroll. We made our way to the side of the Pantheon where the lift had stood earlier in the day. To our sheer horror, it was gone. In utter disbelief, we wondered if the job had been completed earlier in the day. Were we a day late and a dollar short or was this someone's way of telling us that this was an unbelievably bad idea? Our plan was not going well and we had not even started to execute it. With all the checking, double checking, and triple checking we had done to make sure our scheme went off without a hitch, we never considered that the job would be completed and the lift would be moved away.

We stood in the spot where we had planned to make our ascent and discussed how we could get up there. We continued to walk along the brick wall and once we rounded the corner, there sat the lift, parked with tape and pylons surrounding it. Amazed at our good luck, we were initially speechless and unable to move. We were emotionally exhausted by our near miss but it never occurred to us that we did not have to go through with the plan. We could leave right now, enjoy what was left of our week and go home with a remarkable story that would live on in family lore. But not us. Instead, we realized that the revised position of the lift was actually in a better location for our mission. Being in a narrow alleyway, it would be less conspicuous. I reached in my pocket and pulled out the key that I had painstakingly cut. Carefully, I slipped it into the ignition but it would only go part way in. After two more attempts, I realized that my efforts were futile. Having had keys cut over the years, I knew that even those done by a professional do not always initially work. They sometimes have to be recut and refined.

Clare innocently asked, "What's wrong?"

I glared at her but tried to control my frustration. Without speaking, I reached into the backpack and found the small file. I reinserted the key and paid close attention to how far it entered the opening. Once I pulled it out, I noticed a small imperfection in my handiwork and filed the material away. My next attempt was successful. The key went in all the way and when I turned it in the ignition, it activated the control panel. I quickly pressed the silence alarm to keep it from beeping. We had come this far; failure was not an option at this point. After we quickly and quietly entered the cage, I once again inserted the key into the upper control panel, pressed the toggle and we could feel ourselves rising.

"This is so cool," Clare whispered. "This is what you construction guys do all day? Do you just ride up and down in these things? I'm in the wrong line of work."

She seemed far more composed than I was. My heart was racing and I was not sure if what I was feeling was utter exhilaration or sheer panic. Whatever was going on with me, I did not want Clare to pick up on it so I quietly answered with a quick no and did not elaborate. Clare seemed to understand that I was not in a joking frame of mind and did not press the issue.

We reached the rooftop in silence and stepped out of the cage. There was a spectacular view of the city from this vantage point. For a moment, the reason I had this spectacular view slipped my mind. We quickly regrouped and realized that right in front of us were the stairs to the dome ledge. We crouched down and slowly made our way over to them. We took a quick look around to ensure we were not visible. We first moved to the base, and then moved to the steps that lead to the actual dome access. The stairs did not have handrails and appeared incredibly intimidating. We had rehearsed the ascent and proceeded according to plan. We would not stand; rather we would lay low and use baby like moves to get up the stairs. I could feel my heart beating as we slowly made our way up, concentrating on every move. Relief does not begin to describe how we felt when we finally reached the opening fifteen minutes later. After quietly making sure that one another was all right, we looked into the dark abyss of the rotunda. We would have to quickly get what we came for and get out. We noticed that the moonlight only revealed part of the interior dome and that our shadows appeared on one of the panels.

I carefully pulled the knapsack off my back and reached in for the drone and flashlight. There was a slight breeze that helped cool my sweating face. I set the flashlight down close to Clare and I extended the drone's rotors. Clare held the drone as I activated it. Suddenly, we heard the familiar whirling sound. I maneuvered it from Clare's hands and sent it to the opening. Clare pointed the flashlight towards the dome. It illuminated a spectacular array of features. The view was amazing. I had to remind myself that I was not here to sightsee, and to focus on the task at hand. Clare aimed the flashlight at the third row and followed it around that row to the panel. I carefully maneuvered the drone down into the large open space. Clare had to take different positions around the opening and as she moved the light around, I was surprised to see that there were more mysterious markings visible. It seemed like there were a series of them. The LED light was creating sharper images than what the sun was able to expose. I positioned the drone about five feet from the images and started taking snap shots and video footage using my paired phone as a viewer. We worked as a well synchronized team. Clare would slowly move the light and I would follow with the drone and record. We counted six images on the third row of panels, one about every sixth panel. Shining the light on the other panels did not produce any images. Our mission was completed within twenty minutes.

We returned the drone and flashlight to my backpack and smiled at one another with a sense of satisfaction that we had accomplished this far-fetched and painstakingly intricate task. It was now time to work our way down the stairs, out of the Pantheon, and back into the Roman evening air. We knew that descending would be more of a challenge than ascending, so we tried to steady ourselves and not look at what lay beneath us on our way down. We managed to make it onto the waiting lift without incident and started on our way down to Mother Earth. Suddenly, in the quiet of the night we could hear the pulsating siren of the Carbonari. As the sound grew louder, our hearts started beating faster, and our anxiety grew exponentially. When the cage stopped on the ground, we pulled the key from the panel, and quickly scrambled out of it. Once on the ground, we instinctively pulled off our dark outerwear so as not to draw suspicion to ourselves. We stuffed it in the backpack and nonchalantly walked away from the building in the opposite direction from where we initially came. We hoped that we looked like two people in love, out for a midnight stroll in beautiful Rome.

Suddenly, the police car came screeching into the piazza. The flashing blue lights lit up the building and the surrounding area. The car swerved to avoid hitting us, raced past us, and sped off down a narrow street. Although we were trying to hold ourselves steady, our legs were weak and it was all we could do not to collapse in a puddle on the pavement. After the initial shock wore off, we steadied ourselves and took deep breaths to calm our nerves. We quickly moved from unbelievable fright to uncontrollable laughter.

I looked at Clare and said, "I think I just aged ten years."

She replied, "I think I need a diaper change."

Although the situation was not funny at all, we just kept laughing. Every word that either one of us uttered was followed by laughter from the other. Tears were running down our faces, and we could barely walk in a straight line. If anyone saw us, they would have thought that we were a couple of old drunks that had escaped from an asylum. Later, I realized that it must have been hysteria taking over and it was our bodies' defense mechanisms kicking in, protecting us from dissolving into puddles of fear.

We finally returned to our room exhausted, but unscathed from our dangerous mission. We changed, unpacked, and uploaded the videos and pictures from the drone to my laptop. We excitedly sat down, opened the file, and started to examine the images which were of excellent quality. The pictures were sharper and more distinguishable than my father's old video but still faint. The five images that we had recorded were similar in appearance to those that appeared on my father's recording. The symbols, lines and strokes were the same. We could not understand the significance of these markings. Why were there six sets? I recalled from my search back home that the numeral six was thought to be a perfect number, much like the number twenty-eight. The plot was thickening for us amateur detectives, and our findings only raised more questions than answers. It was nearly daylight, and we decided that it was time to put our ill-gotten information away for the night and try to sleep. There had been enough excitement for one day and we somehow had to turn off our adrenaline taps. We showered, toasted our success with a small shot of grappa and crawled into bed tightly holding one another.

Once asleep, my mind must have still been in high gear because my dream did not end as well as our evening did. In my nightmare we were running as the police chased us down narrow alleys and up steps through villas and onto rooftops. We were surrounded by Italian police yelling at us to surrender as we continued to allude them. Clare screamed out to me to go this way and we leaped from a parapet into a dumpster filled with the day's refuse. The smelly, slimy discards covered us. The only sound we could hear was the police running past us frantically searching every dark opening. We sat motionless in the discarded food waste. Any slight move or sneeze could rattle the garbage and alert the police. Just when we thought we were safe in our dark little world of zucchini peels, artichoke hearts and onion skins, the light of three flashlights shined on us.

Someone yelled, "Andiamo!"

I remembered that word from my childhood. My mother would yell that to me when I would drag my heels getting out of bed on school days. I knew that it meant they wanted us to get out of the dumpster and go with them. And that meant we were in trouble. We crawled out of the metal box and into the police car and were then transported to the station and locked in adjoining cells. At the jail, the only comfort we had was that we could hold one another's hands through the metal bars for reassurance. I looked at Clare and apologized for dragging her into this crazy misadventure.

Somehow, her sense of humor was still intact. She looked at me and said, "This isn't going to look good on a resume."

I replied, "We will not need a resume. They will send us to St. Helena and poison us to death like Napoleon."

We laughed. We decided that we had to look at the humor in the situation to keep ourselves sane, regardless of how dark the humor may be.

The prison guard soon entered with a silver platter holding crystal champagne glasses filled with Prosecco and an antipasto plate arranged on fine porcelain dinnerware. It was brimming with capicola, olives, cheese, and crusty bread just like my mother made. He spread a woven red checkered cloth over the table and arranged a place-setting for two. He then unlocked our cells and motioned for us to sit down at the table and eat. We sat and he placed napkins on our laps. In broken English he asked if there was anything else he could get us.

When I asked him if they treat all prisoners like this in Italy, he replied, "Ah, Signore, consider this your last supper. It is a tradition here. We are not barbarians and we want you to enjoy the last moments of your life."

I looked at him incredulously and responded, "Are you kidding me? We did not steal anything or harm anyone."

He nodded his head in agreement and said, "I understand, but you did violate very sacred ground without a Papal permit to do so. This is punishable by death."

I woke up screaming and in a cold sweat. I startled Clare out of her sleep and recounted the dream with all the vivid detail that I could remember. She said that is why it was a good thing that we did not get caught and drifted back to sleep.

Despite my distressing dream, I awoke feeling refreshed and ready to take our mission to the next level. After a quick shower and a trip to the café, we returned to our room and dived deep into our discovery from the night before. We once again looked at the images that we had captured. I numbered each picture based on its location. Image one was 3-1-28, image two was 3-2-28 continuing up to 3-6-28. The three signified the third row up, the next number represented the position one through six and the twenty-eight was the number of panels in the row. Next, we took each image and rotated them one by one to see if we could find a clue as to the orientation or the symbol's significance. There did not seem to be an obvious explanation. We then tried to match them up like a puzzle by trying different combinations. This proved to be a painstaking and frustrating process only to find no obvious connection.

There had to be something significant about them. There must be a reason that someone would bother to etch the panels in such a way.

We tried shading the markings in assorted colors and expanding and contracting the size. I searched all the alphabets of the world, both ancient and current to see if there were any matches. We used every editing tool we had in the photoshop software. Nothing worked. These etchings must have been created for a specific reason. We had to be missing something and I was determined to find it. I could not accept that we came all this way, wasted all this time and expense, and most importantly, risked our lives to produce nothing but a random bunch of symbols and markings that have no meaning. We spent hours trying to make sense of the markings.

I looked at Clare and said, "Someone, somewhere, somehow should be able to translate this stuff for us."

She suggested that we search the web for ancient Roman alphabets but once again, we found absolutely nothing. We moved onto ancient Greek and then ancient Egyptian alphabets. Occasionally we would find a match but they were never exactly the same. We surmised that it could be an attempt by an illiterate artisan trying to memorialize his workmanship and leave a message for posterity. Or it could be a note left by a worker that had created his own alphabet or language such as Pig Latin. This actually made a bit of sense. After all the written word is man's greatest invention. Without it there would not have been industrialization and the resultant prosperity that brought us our modern world. We concluded that there did not seem to be any logical interpretation of the markings but we were sure that they meant something. And I was determined to find out what it was.

Suddenly Clare said, "Who owns the building? My guess is that whoever it is must have inherited its contents. I suspect the Vatican may have information in their secret library."

As usual, she had a good point and we decided to follow up on it. We discovered that the Vatican secret library or the Vatican Apostolic Archives is off limits to almost everyone except for a chosen few. It contains one of the world's largest archives of ancient documents but to have access, there were requirements, none of which qualified us. A person had to be seventy-five years old and a scholar and they had to be recertified every six months. Research could not exceed three pre-requested documents per day, taking pictures was forbidden, and materials could not be removed from the library. The building was guarded by Swiss soldiers who escorted visitors to their seat. Unfortunately, we did not know any seventy-five-year-old scholars, so we would have to once again tap into our stealth skills to gain access. Compared to our Pantheon maneuvers, this would be a cake walk. Without a plan in hand and no time to waste, we made our way to the Vatican. We strolled through the narrow alleys past the shops, cafes, restaurants, and vendors selling their wares. On a regular vacation this would have captured our interest but today we were on a mission. Absorbing and enjoying the local culture was off the table today.

We arrived at the Vatican and decided that despite the urgent purpose of our visit, we could not leave without visiting St. Peter's Basilica. As we entered the square, we were in awe of the grandiose building and the wall of curved columns that supported it. We made our way to the Basilica and entered its sacred walls. The enormity was breath taking. The artwork that adorned every inch of the building was overwhelming. We stopped and paid our respects at St. Peter's alter. Before leaving the Basilica, we headed to the gift shop and browsed the artifacts and trinkets just like any typical tourist, forgetting why we were really there.

Afterwards, we visited the Sistine Chapel to view the works of Michelangelo. It was stunning. We imagined the room filled with scaffolding and Michelangelo laying on his back placing brush strokes of paint onto the ceiling. We could not fathom the amount of time that it must have taken to complete the project. He was a man dedicated to his art and a man well ahead of his time. Had he lived in our modern world and had access to the technology of today, it is unimaginable what his accomplishments could have been. He was truly a renaissance man, who through his wisdom, talent and intelligence enhanced the generation of his time.

All too soon, our hasty sightseeing tour was over and we moved on to the Vatican Library. There we found more exquisite sculptures and architecture, but no books that we could access. The only point of entry was through well-guarded gates. We realized that there was no way for us to breach the walls and browse the library. We approached the person sitting behind the desk and asked how we could access information about the Pantheon. In particularly good English he told us that the documents had been digitized and are now available online. He handed us a pamphlet that contained information about the website. I quickly scanned it and thanked him. He told us that the Pantheon was under the jurisdiction of The Ministry of Cultural Heritage and Activities and Tourism. He suggested that we visit their offices and he proceeded to sketch us a map. Remarkedly, it was close to our hotel and within walking distance of The Pantheon. We thanked him and proceeded with the next leg of our journey.

We quickly moved through the cobble stone streets and arrived at their headquarters. Once we were inside the main lobby, we approached the front desk and explained that we were researching the Pantheon and were wondering if we would be able to review any archives that would be available. He asked to see our identification, carefully reviewed it, and then told us to go down the hall, turn left and near the end of that hall we would find the Office of Archives. I thanked him with my limited Italian and we headed towards our destination. Upon entering, we found a room filled with books and documents and standing before us, was the keeper of information. We once again explained the purpose of our visit and told him that we were hoping to find information regarding its construction. The clerk told us that there is extremely limited information available and then led us to a shelf. He told us that everything they had would be found there in an accordion file. To our dismay, documents and drawings were scarce. Carefully, we scanned each piece of paper. Everything in the file appeared to be copies of original documents. There were sketches and writings of ancient Roman literature. I took pictures of the documents, returned the file, and we made our way to the street.

We decided to head back to our room and try to decipher the information, but not before we stopped to eat. Food is usually a big part of our lives and our travels, but on this trip, it had become something that we had to squeeze into our day. We decided to stop and enjoy our lunch rather than just eat something out of physical need. We chose eggplant parmigiana paired with Valpolicella wine and a seasonal salad. The main course would be topped off with spumoni gelato. After we finished our meal, we sat under the large umbrella, sipped our wine, and watched people go about their business. Vespas and cars whizzed by as people were moving about the street in no particular hurry. We watched the pigeons pick up scraps of food from the road. For the first time since we landed in Rome, we started to relax and feel like we were on a vacation. We marveled at the glorious day. I felt like I could sit there endlessly and watch modern life move about in this ancient world, but we had work to do and it was time to return to the confines of our room.

Back at the hotel, I once again fired up the computer and started to search through the digitized Vatican Library website. I typed in Pantheon and about a dozen manuscripts appeared on the screen. We looked through page after page, searching for diagrams or sketches that resembled the Pantheon. The pages had handwritten words that I was unable to read, but the level and amount of documentation was impressive. There were rudimentary and colorful detailed diagrams of the building along with landscape and geographic maps. What really captured my imagination were the diagrams depicting the actual methods of construction. The enormous structures that were assembled to transport and lift columns and blocks into place, were simply impressive. I was amazed at how wood was used to make large gears and screws in order to adjust, rotate and lift heavy stone building materials. There were even drawings of portable water wheels that appeared to be used to turn concrete mixers or coil rope around a drum to lift objects. Obviously, there were extraordinarily talented and innovative engineers even in those early days. I found myself drifting off course, fantasizing that if there was a time machine, I would like to go back to those times, even if for just one day. I wished I had the time to have all these documents translated so I could better understand the nature of life in past centuries, but I knew that I needed to regroup and change my focus back to the task at hand. It was going to take hours just to research all the available data.

One of the documents that I was leafing through appeared to be a book of architectural study with detailed sketches of columns, cornices, and monuments. There was a hand drawn rough sketch of the Pantheon with words encircling it. The words were difficult to translate and initially rejected by my translation application, so I had to use my best guess to get the job done. The words seemed to be a description of the structure and what it was made of. It also included basic dimensions and potential theories as to the original purpose and function of the building. It went on to say that the Pantheon bore a significant Greek character and was fashioned after the Acropolis of Athens. It was then that I found what I was looking for. The author made a reference to the interior and the panels. It was mostly regarding size and dimensions but there was one peculiar entry dealing with six panels having suspicious but very faint features. He wrote that these features are only visible at certain times. There was no theory as to how they originated or what they meant, but it did confirm that the markings were there centuries ago.

Next, I searched Marcus Agrippa. He built the Pantheon previous to the one that is now standing. Marcus was a great Roman general and his name remains on the Portico to this day. With this search, I found manuscripts and a diagram that was a cross section of The Pantheon. I leafed through the file filled with life like sketches and drawings of individuals. The manuscript appeared to be a record of bravery and chronicled those who were the bravest. It was likely a textbook used in education. Famous leaders and historically significant players were listed with a drawing of their profile and their names were handwritten in Roman or Greek above their likeness. I was surprised to see drawings of Mark Antony and Cleopatra. Among the drawings were other well-known figures of ancient times such as Caesar, Hippocrates, Socrates and even Hercules.

Next, I moved onto the sectional depiction of The Pantheon. It was drawn in the late 1700s as a record and not as the original design. Once again, it did not hold any clues as to the markings. We kept searching by using different keywords that we thought would connect us to more information. What we found were manuscripts and bibliographies filled with pages of writings and drawings, all in Greek or Roman, none of which we could read. We decided to make one final attempt to find more information by pouring over the pictures we took at the Heritage Office. We opened each file and zoomed in and out looking for whatever added information they might hold. There were drawings and descriptions but nothing significant. If the explanation of what these markings were could not be found in all the pages, we had just spent hours reviewing, it seemed that we were at a dead end. But we had come this far and I was not ready to give up yet. I hoped that Clare felt the same.

Clare was always a steady presence in my life. Even when my world seemed to be spinning out of control, she had this uncanny ability to stand with her feet firmly planted on the ground and weather whatever storm was raging. She was my calm and logic when I needed it. She once described herself as a tree in a storm. Even if her leaves and branches break away, her roots are always firmly planted in the ground. While this was a quality that I admired in my loving, supportive wife, it could also make her difficult to read. My next question would let me know where she really stood on our adventure and just how supportive she actually was.

"Clare, how do you feel about going to Athens?" I asked. "We can fly in tomorrow and see what we can find in their archives. We can catch a morning flight, spend the night, and return to Rome Thursday evening."

To my surprise and relief, she answered, "It sounds doable. We're already here, so why not."

We immediately reserved a 10:00 a.m. flight to Athens, a room at the Hilton, and a flight that would bring us back to Rome by 6:00 p.m. the next day. As we packed for the overnight trip, excitement grabbed ahold of us. This was so out of our comfort zone, but in a crazy way it felt liberating.

Unable to sleep, we decided to close out the night with an evening walk to The Altare della Patria. The white light enveloping the buildings and monuments on this dark night gave the buildings an appearance of stature and prominence. We found a trattoria and once again indulged in Italian cuisine. With a full stomach, and our excitement and anticipation dulled by the physical exercise and fatigue, we headed back to our room for some much-needed sleep.

Chapter V
HELIOS ADVENTURE

The next morning the alarm sounded at 6:00 a.m. and we quickly jumped out of bed, showered and dressed. We dragged our luggage out of the room and down the hall to the elevator.

In the lobby, the concierge greeted us, "Boungiorno Signor e Signora."

I handed him my valet slip and he summoned a young fellow who grabbed the ticket and disappeared around the corner. We stood on the sidewalk, quietly breathing in the morning air. The sun had just risen, but the air was already warm and thick. The streets were starting to show signs of life with people moving about, making their way to work. Seemingly out of nowhere, the blue Fiat appeared in front of us, and the young valet opened the hatch and loaded our bags. I handed him five euros before we got in the car and made our way to the airport. It was a relatively easy drive as we were retracing the route that brought us to Rome. It was when we arrived at the airport that my stress level escalated. The hard part was over and all we had to do was park. It should have been easy, but nothing is easy when stress takes over and panic becomes the normal state of being. Not knowing what lane to stay in, I barked at Clare to look for an airport parking sign.

By the time she saw the sign and pointed it out to me, we missed the turnoff and we had to turn around. I drove tentatively, which attracted the attention and the all too familiar beeping of horns by impatient Romans.

Clare yelled, "Get in the right lane Jim."

My reply reflected my anxious state of mind.

"I'm trying to but the cars won't let me switch lanes. What the hell? Are there no courteous drivers in Rome?" I yelled, exasperated with the situation.

When signaling did not work, I started drifting over to the right lane, hoping that someone would slow down and let me in to avoid being hit. My plan B worked and I managed to get onto the off ramp just in time to enter the airport parking area. We both gave a huge sigh of relief.

I looked at Clare and stated the obvious, "We should have taken a cab. I hate driving to airports."

It seemed like every airport that I have been through has the same problem. No matter how hard the planners try to make it easy to maneuver on airport property, it always seems like a botched-up tangle of roads with signs that show up way too late to exit to a ramp. But if I am being honest with myself, it could just be me.

Entering the garage and making payment was easy. The gate rose and we entered the multi-tiered structure filled with what I surmised was hundreds of vehicles. All we had to do was find a spot to park. We drove through row after row until we were almost at the roof.

Suddenly Clare shouted, "There is one over there."

I stepped on the gas so no one could beat me to the spot. Our mission was successful. We parked and before getting out of the car, I stopped and took a couple deep breaths in an effort to regroup. It is never an easy, uneventful drive to the airport. I agonize about every detail from being too early, to being too late, and would we find a parking spot? Clare has said that I set up a mental obstacle course for myself. If I could just relax, the trip would go more smoothly. She says that when my anxiety escalates, my brain simultaneously shuts down. I know that she is right, but unfortunately, I do the same thing over and over again. I apologized to Clare for the way I spoke to her. She said she understood, but it was not all right. She admonished me and told me that I have to do better in the future. I assured her that I would. My intention was always to do better, but I knew there was a very slim chance that it would happen. It was just the way that I was built.

We quickly made our way to the terminal dragging our bags behind us. Whoever designed wheels on luggage was my hero that day. We arrived at the check-in and displayed our electronic tickets and our passports. We placed our carry-on bags onto the conveyor belt and stepped through the metal detector. There were no problems and we were on our way to the gate. We were a bit early so we grabbed ourselves a coffee, and then sat down and waited with the rest of the tourists. After about an hour, boarding began. After a quick two-hour flight, we landed in Greece.

Once we were inside the terminal, we headed straight to the taxi stand. Within minutes we were on our way to our hotel in downtown Athens. The city is low rise and like Rome, there are cars parked in every available spot on the streets. The houses and buildings are light colored and show their age. The streets are beautifully lined with trees providing much needed shade. We pulled up to our hotel and a young man helped us out of the taxi. I paid the driver, and we headed to the check-in desk.

"Geia sas," I said, greeting the clerk with my best Rosetta Stone Greek.

She smiled, paused for a moment, and replied in fluent English. It was obvious that my attempt in linguistics was once again a failure. She checked us in, handed us our keycards and pointed us to the elevator. Once inside our room we unpacked and set up the computer. There was no time to rest. I found a map of the city and located where the archives were. A computer search showed that the Greek National Archives were about a forty-five-minute walk from the hotel. That was perfect. The walk should burn off any of my remaining stress and afterwards we could relax and enjoy our stay in Greece. We slipped into our sneakers and made our way out to the bustling street.

About fifteen minutes into our trek, we decided to duck into one of the local open-air restaurants. The hostess greeted us and motioned us to a comfortable seating area with a view of the street. I told her we only speak English and she responded in kind, saying she hoped we enjoy our stay and made suggestions on how to avoid tourist traps. We told her that we were heading to the archives and this was going to be our late lunch. She gave us our menus and then explained what all the items were. After going over the massive selection of foods, we chose a simple lunch of olives, tzatziki, and moussaka with a glass of Greek beer. She took our order and quickly returned with our beverages. We clinked our glasses and toasted ourselves for being so adventurous.

I looked at Clare and asked, "Isn't this fun?"

She answered, "You know what? In a crazy way it is. At first, I thought you were a bit nuts about this whole thing but I'm starting to enjoy it. Now I know how all those travel experts feel about the places they explore. It's both exciting and educational."

We basked in the warm Greek breeze sipping our beer until our food arrived. We savored every bite and cleaned every morsel from our plates. We then paid our tab and thanked the hostess for her guidance and hospitality. Once again, we were on our way to the Archives. Closely following our GPS, we turned down narrow streets, walking through parks and past monuments bearing the busts of local heroes. The buildings were adorned with the blue Greek flag. After another thirty-five-minutes, we arrived at the National Archives. We entered the white marble, ultra-modern structure. Tourists filled the lobby, waiting to see what marvels the building held.

We politely approached the gentleman at the front counter and I said, "Excuse me sir, we are here to do some research and we were wondering if we could browse through some of your documents."

The gentleman pointed to where the catalogues were located and told us that from there, we could determine where to find the information we needed. We thanked him and made our way to the area he directed us to. There, we found records associated with the Acropolis and the Parthenon. This seemed like a good start since the Pantheon portico was similar to the Parthenon.

We learned that the Acropolis and Parthenon dated back to around 430 BCE. Pericles commissioned the structures and hired two well-known architects, Callicrates and Ictinus for the build. The Parthenon, being a much older building, played a significant role in the design of the Pantheon with one major distinction. The Pantheon has the circular domed structure which the Parthenon does not have. It is only the portico that resembles the Pantheon. There was little more information that we could glean from the archives. After a couple of hours of searching through documents and drawings we saw no point in carrying on. We had hit another dead end. Discouraged, we headed back towards our hotel. We decided that we could not allow the disappointing research to stop us from doing a bit of sightseeing. We approached the desk clerk who recommended that we visit the Acropolis where the night show is fabulous. He told us that we would not be disappointed.

The history of the Acropolis is one of centuries of construction, dynasties, battles, empires, and rebirth. The beginning of philosophy is credited to Socrates who walked among the ruins back in mid-400 BCE only to be executed for trying to enlighten the youth of his era. Greece played a major cultural role through the ages, and is still influencing our modern world through literature, art, and architecture. We took a taxi to the ruins and were completely enthralled by its enormity. The Acropolis is situated on a massive rock high above the city. In ancient times, locating your fortification high above the surrounding land was a strategic method of defense from attackers. We paid our entrance fee and walked the ruins as the sun began to set. We were in awe of the beauty of the night as we strolled the limestone and marble antiquities trying to imagine throngs of ancient Greeks seated in the amphitheater listening to a wise philosopher.

We moved on to the Parthenon and its stately columns. Scaffolding surrounded parts of the structure. One can only imagine the effort that it took to build this massive temple which once housed the statue of Athena. I thought back to my days in college when we studied the assorted styles of column capitals and the eras they represented. The three periods were the Doric, the Ionic and the Corinthian. The Doric style was the simplest with no decorative attributes while the Ionic had the scrolled looking capital, and finally the Corinthian which had the most complex, decorative style depicting leaves on its capital. The capitals of the Parthenon are characteristic of the Doric style, while the Pantheon is characterized by the more intricate Corinthian style of column.

It was awe inspiring to see the actual Parthenon. The Greek Revival style of architecture was brought to America by Thomas Jefferson when he incorporated it in his home at Monticello. America embraced this type of design and built government buildings in the Greek style. One of the major reasons we were drawn to this style of architecture was the symbol of democracy that Greece represented. It was also an homage to their arts and education. The closest we had previously come to seeing it was the full-sized replica that stands in Nashville Tennessee complete with Athena's forty-foot-high statue. Being here in Greece, touring the original Parthenon, we realized that the replica does not do it justice at all.

The nighttime lighting and the glow from the interior of the temple highlighted the columns. The scene was both surreal and breathtaking. We slowly walked around the building absorbing its grandiose splendor. After taking snapshots at strategic locations and angles, we took the obligatory selfie, returned to the entrance, and called for an uber. Driving through the streets of Athens at night is an experience of its own. We asked the driver to take us to Monastiraki Square, a popular tourist stop in Athens. The moment we were dropped off we were immediately immersed in Greek nightlife. Revelers were moving from bar to bar as street artists were performing their routines for attentive audiences. We stopped for a moment to watch a juggler, and then moved on to a violinist, each time dropping a euro or two in their waiting containers.

The party atmosphere took me back to my youthful days, going out with my friends, getting rowdy and hoping to attract female attention. Those days were history, and now the married version of myself was here with Clare to take part in Athens' nightlife in a different, more mature manner. We entered a restaurant and were seated next to a table of four couples who appeared to be out on the town to eat, drink and be merry. We seated ourselves and ordered ouzo, the drink of Greece. We tried to block the reveling and merriment that surrounded us long enough to decide what we should order. Based on the help we received at lunch we easily made our choices and sat back to soak in the environment. We must have caught the attention of the table next to us. A woman stood up and approached our table. She greeted us and asked where we were from. We introduced ourselves and she invited us to slide our table over and join them. The rest of the group cheered us and made a toast to Greece, America and surprisingly to Nashville Tennessee. Apparently, it is no secret that the Parthenon replica is housed there.

After our food arrived, we pushed it to the center of the table as the plan was for everyone to share their selection. Even though they were strangers to us, it felt like a family gathering filled with laughter and endless conversation. We were immersed in the country's easy-going culture and we loved it. We were asked about our home, our family and what brought us to Athens. The friendly conversation went back and forth and seemed effortless and endless. We were as intrigued by the lives of the people we were sharing our meal with as they were with us.

Hours passed before we bid them good night. We could see that the streets were still filled with revelers and the energy was both palpable and addictive but it was getting late and we were feeling the strain of the day's activities. We hated to leave our new friends but we realized that it was time to go. As we rose from the table, we expressed our warmest gratitude to our new friends for inviting us to join them and making us a part of a wonderful evening. We approached each person, and one by one we bid them adieu and happiness. They responded warmly with either a hug or a handshake.

Returning to the square, still on an emotional high and a bit inebriated, we realized that we had a good half hour walk to our hotel so we decided that we had enough exercise for the day and summoned a taxi. By the time we were back in our room, we were exhausted but felt that we still needed to make some time to go over the results of the day one last time. We concluded that the Pantheon designers must have visited Athens to get ideas for their prospective structure and other than that a connection between the Parthenon and the Pantheon did not exist. We may have struck out on the information front but we had an evening soaked in Greek culture that we would remember.

We decided to leave earlier than planned and managed to book a 10:00 a.m. flight to Rome. With our plans complete, I moved towards the bed and impulsively took one of the pillows and smashed it into Clare's face. I do not know what possessed me. Maybe the exuberance of the night was still with me or maybe I was still a bit drunk, but it seemed like the perfect time to have a pillow fight. She quickly grabbed the other pillow and threw it at me but missed as I ducked to avoid the projectile. I declared a truce while I was ahead. She agreed and then sat on me and bashed me with the pillow a couple of times. Laughing, she told me to surrender or I sleep on the couch. We were so pumped up from the excitement of the evening that it was doubtful we would be able to sleep. Remarkably, we dozed off in the sumptuous bed pretty much as soon as our heads hit the pillow.

The 6:00 a.m. alarm announced that morning had arrived. We moaned and struggled to get out of bed. Once again, we showered and packed and headed to the lobby for coffee and a quick breakfast. After paying for the room, we walked to the front entrance where taxis were lined up waiting for passengers and I was able to flag one of the vehicles. The driver quickly loaded our belongings into the trunk and we were on our way back to the airport. As the route passed through pleasant tree lined neighborhoods, I found myself thinking that this was so much more relaxing than making the drive myself. At the airport, we paid our fare and headed to the check-in desk. With robotic precision we were subjected to all the usual checks and inspections prior to making our way to the gate.

Seeing the azure blue Adriatic Sea and the mountains from above was spectacular. The flight ended quickly and before we knew it, we were once again in Rome. We disembarked and made our way through the terminal towards the parking lot. Safe, in the bowels of the massive parking structure sat our little blue Fiat, waiting to return us to our hotel. There was no urgency to contend with on the drive back to the room, so the traffic jams, honking horns and hand jesters meant for slow or indecisive drivers were not irritating. After an uneventful drive, we arrived at the hotel and we handed our car over to the valet.

Back in our room we unpacked and decided to go for lunch. By now we were savvy Roman tourists. We felt comfortable entering the streets and searching out a good lunch spot. A bit of prosciutto, cheese, artichokes, and a fresh Mediterranean salad consisting of tomatoes, cucumbers, lettuce, and olives appealed to our culinary senses. A glass of wine and a slice of stone oven bread rounded out the menu. After devouring the last bit of salad, we sat trying to unwind before paying the bill and heading back to the hotel.

Chapter VI
CYBER WARS

After a short walk, we made our way up to our room, and laid down on the bed for a much-needed break. We chatted about how amazing our trip had been. Within minutes, I moved from the bed and seated myself in front of the laptop. So much for rest. While waiting for the computer to load, I made a pot of coffee. I knew that Clare would appreciate a nice warm mug of brew. When I returned to the computer the home screen was dark with unrecognizable Italian words scrolling across it. I hit the return key and nothing happened. Next, I tried the escape key, and then the delete key but had the same result. The screen and the message stayed the same.

I called Clare over to the computer and said in a panic, "Look at this."

"That does not look good," she replied in her calm, understated way.

I immediately shifted to panic mode and replied, "No shit, Captain Obvious. What the hell is going on here?"

The utter terror I was feeling could not be contained. I continued tapping different keys hoping for a different result, but nothing changed.

By now my panic had turned to frenzy and I screamed, "Damn it! This is why I hate connecting to hotel WIFI."

I jotted down the words flashing across the screen and entered them in the translation application on my phone. The now recognizable words elevated my panicked state of mind to sheer distress.

It read, *your computer has been kidnapped and we want ten thousand euros to give it back. Press the caps lock and backspace together for further instructions.*

I did as I was instructed and another message appeared.

The translation read; *You have until midnight tonight to deliver ten thousand euros.*

Then the screen started to change color and another message appeared. This time the instructions detailed how and when to send the ransom money through a local wire transfer office.

My mind was in overdrive as I desperately tried to steady myself. I realized that we have run into this problem at work and the person to call and potentially help me get out of this mess was Rajish, our IT wizard.

I dialed his cell phone and he immediately picked up and said, "Hi Jim. I am surprised to see your number pop up on my phone. Aren't you on vacation?"

"I am, but I have a problem. We are in Rome and my computer has been hacked with ransomware. Can you help me remotely? I know you have dealt with this in the past," I said trying to sound calm.

He asked if I had my company laptop with me. When I told him that I did, he said he could find my IP address in our records. He said he would see what he could do and he would get back to me. I told him to hurry because the ransom threat was time sensitive and would expire at midnight. He told me that it would be his next and only course of business and he assured me that I would hear from him shortly.

While we waited for his call, Clare and I searched our phones for any Italian authorities that may be able to help us. We discovered that this sort of thing happens quite a bit and that Italy has a department called Guardia di Finanza who deal exclusively with these types of crimes. Within minutes, my phone rang and Rajish started to explain what he had uncovered. He told me that he sourced my IP address and could see the messages that I received remotely. He said the computer sending them was located at the Central Library of Rome. He surmised that we were dealing with low level hackers who were not too sophisticated because good, professional hackers would be much harder to trace. He said there was no guarantee they would remain at that location, so he would keep monitoring the computer's movements.

He then said, "Jim, next time use the virtual private network."

Apologetically, I replied, "Rajish, I should know better and I have no excuse. I am usually incredibly careful, but unfortunately, I let my guard down and got stung. This has been a valuable lesson. Hopefully, we can come out of this unscathed."

I thanked him and told him to keep me posted if he had any additional information. In the meantime, we would be going to the authorities to see what they could do to help us at this end of the world. When I called the Guardia di Finanza an actual human being promptly answered the phone. I explained to the person on the line what had just happened and proceeded to say that I had valuable information as to the source. The person told me to hold while they transferred me to one of their agents. After a brief wait, I found myself talking to a gentleman named Giovanni who asked me what the problem was. Once again, I explained who I was, what had happened and our IT person's findings. He asked if we could come to the office with the computer. I told him that we were on our way because the ransomware expired at midnight and I would lose all my data if we were to delay.

I quickly packed up the computer, and Clare and I headed down to the street. We flagged a taxi and instructed the driver to take us to the address that the agent gave me. It took an extremely long half hour to reach our destination. Every stoplight was a source of frustration. Every slowdown in traffic was cause for anxiety. We could not get there soon enough. The building we arrived at was a nondescript limestone six story structure completely surrounded by impenetrable fencing. We paid our fare, hopped out and ran to the gated entrance. We gave the guard both of our names and the agent's name that was expecting us. He picked up the phone, uttered unrecognizable Italian words, hung up, and cleared us for entrance. He gave us directions and we scurried down a hallway filled with photos of outstanding agents and their awards. We made a sharp left turn and we quickly found Giovanni's office. He must have been watching us on camera because he opened the door before we knocked.

Once inside, he greeted us warmly in English and said "Except for this problem, I hope you are enjoying your visit to Rome. I apologize for this horrible situation. No one wants to be the victim of a crime when they are on holiday."

He asked to look at the computer. I pulled it out, plugged it in and the message appeared on the screen.

He looked at it, paused and said, "This is a new one. We have not seen this one before. It is probably a new character or perhaps a novice looking to make quick easy money since your computer expert was able to trace the source so easily. In most cases it is almost impossible to trace the culprit. They are usually very sophisticated. This is a lucky break for you. I believe we can take care of this quickly."

He picked up his phone and called another agent who appeared at the door within minutes. The two engaged in an intense rapid-fire discussion in Italian. The second agent left and Giovanni explained that they would arrange for a team to go to the library and pick up the person responsible for the ransomware. He explained that they would apprehend the suspect by surprise so he could not crash his computer and destroy its contents. He said that would be our best chance at getting our information back. The plan was to infiltrate the library with undercover agents that appear to be people looking at books and documents. This would distract the perpetrator from the actual agents that would be tasked with the takedown. He explained that once they identify the individual they would carefully move in and arrest him before he could make a move. One of their well-trained technology agents would then access the computer, unlock the information and we would then have our data back.

I said with relief, "That sounds great. What would you like us to do?"

"Go back to your room and wait for my call. But before you go I will need you to provide information so I can file and record the case," he said.

We complied, thanked Giovanni, and left the station. Once we were outside we waited for a taxi to arrive. It was during these few minutes that I totally derailed the plan that the agent had laid before us.

I looked at Clare and said, "We should go to the library and watch what happens. I can't just sit and wait."

She agreed and we gave the taxi driver the library address instead of the address for the hotel. After about twenty-five minutes we were at our destination. We approached the contemporary glass structure and entered the grand lobby that was adorned with fascinating displays and visual effects. We made our way to an upper floor where we found row upon row of shelves laden with books. We knew we had to remain inconspicuous, so we devised a plan. I would pretend to be browsing in the rows of books, while Clare would grab one and sit down. As I moved myself through the aisles, I would keep an eye on the people sitting down, looking at their computers.

On the first floor, other than students that looked like they were doing group work, there was nothing that stood out as suspicious. I made eye contact with Clare and moved up to the next level of the library. Once I was situated in the racks, Clare appeared and nonchalantly found herself a place to sit and review a random book. Nothing looked suspicious, so once again I nodded to Clare and I made my way up to the next floor. There were people sitting at desks peering into their laptops. I headed for the bookshelves and started my fake search. By this time, Clare once again appeared with books in her arms and sat down at a desk.

I decided to move to a position among the shelves of books that had a better vantage point. There, I noticed a woman who appeared to be browsing but was taking occasional glances at computers while reaching for books on the shelf. This had to be one of the agents. Over at the desks, I noticed a person look up and tug at his earlobe while looking directly at a young man sitting at a desk with a well-protected screen and a great deal of open space surrounding him. Could this be the suspect deliberately sitting there in case he needed to make an escape? Minutes ticked away as adrenalin pumped through my body. In my mind, I imagined various scenarios of how the take down would play out. I was tempted to casually wander in his direction to see if he would abruptly shut down his computer, but I decided not to because I knew that could blow the whole operation.

I then noticed the woman grab a book and place herself as close to the individual as possible without looking obvious or suspicious. She sat down, read a bit, and started taking notes. The individual behind the laptop appeared oblivious to what was slowly transpiring. What felt like hours had passed with nothing happening. I could only assume this was a technique to normalize the atmosphere so the suspect is at ease with his surroundings. Without warning, the woman dropped her pen and rolled it towards the person immersed in his computer screen. He seemed to notice the pen approach his desk. He bent down, picked it up and appeared to stand up to return the pen. Suddenly there was a flurry of activity. The woman grabbed him and put him into a hold while another agent attempted to handcuff him. The suspect wrestled himself free and ran towards the exit. While one agent gave chase, the other agent rushed to the computer, sat down, and started tapping away on the keyboard. No longer needing to blend into the woodwork, I ran over to the window and watched as the man ran across the parking lot and jumped into a black vehicle. The agent had by this time been joined by another officer. They jumped in a vehicle and gave chase. I memorized the license plate number as it sped off.

I approached the person working on the computer, explained who I was and gave him the escapee's plate number and a description of the car. He immediately reached for his phone and called the information in. Within minutes I could hear the wail of police sirens. He then looked up at me and said that my computer should be all right now. I thanked him profusely. There were no words to express the gratitude and relief that I felt for the swift and effective action they took to save the data on my computer. We shook hands and I walked away from the officer and over to Clare.

We sat down and booted up the computer. I immediately connected to the VPN, and then shut it down and headed out of the building into the misty dusk. Emotionally exhausted, we hailed a taxi and sat in silence for the entire twenty-five-minute ride. At this point, we were catatonic from the shock of what we had just lived through and what could have happened if the perpetrator had not been caught.

After returning to our room my phone rang. It was Giovanni calling to inform me that after a chase through the streets of Rome, the individual was surrounded by the police and captured without incident. He said we were extremely fortunate that he was a low-level criminal with little experience in this type of activity. He said that hopefully with time in jail and time to reflect he would learn that crime does not pay and he would seek out a legitimate way to make a living. He acknowledged that times were tough and everyone was looking for a fast and effortless way to prosper. Unfortunately, robbing industrious individuals of their legally gotten gains was not the way to do it. He obviously had no sympathy for the young man. He reminded me that if I log into the VPN I should not have any further problems.

I once again thanked him for his quick and efficient assistance and bid him, "Ciao."

After the call ended, I turned to Clare and said, "I need a drink. How about if we grab a bite to eat and wash it down with a bottle of wine? A drunken stupor might snap me out of this state of shock."

Without hesitation, Clare yelled, "Andiamo!"

We shut the computer down and headed to the street. We decided that pizza and a bottle or two of Valpolicella wine would be a comforting way to end the tumultuous day. The pizza arrived in short order and we inhaled it without even touching the wine. We were ravenous and did not even know it. Afterwards, we clinked our first glass of wine and started to sip the glorious tasting liquid.

I looked at Clare and said, "You know, our work is done here and we don't know any more about the markings than when we left home. What should we do next? Should we forget about the Pantheon, knowing that we gave it our best effort and just enjoy Rome for the time that we have left here?"

Clare responded in her typical, logical fashion, "I don't want to think about it tonight. I just want to unwind and enjoy this lovely evening. We can talk about it tomorrow."

As always, my anchor in life was right. We finished the wine, paid the bill, and left the restaurant arm in arm. We decided to explore the city with no particular purpose and no specific destination. We stopped, looked at one another, smiled, hugged, and kissed. This is what a romantic vacation should feel like.

After taking in a couple of the Old Roman town antiquities we made our way back to the hotel room. Unfortunately, the wine had muddled our brains and we had lost our sense of direction. After aimlessly walking down street after street we finally saw familiar sites. Eventually we found our way back to the hotel. The room and the computer were intact. All was right in the world. A sense of peace and calm had been restored. There were no plans for the next day and the alarm was not set. We dropped onto the bed and instantly fell into a deep, blissful sleep.

Chapter VII
FIRENZA

The next morning arrived with the usual sounds of the city's hustle and bustle below. It was 7:00 a.m. and beams of sunlight were streaming into the room between the curtains. We awoke wearing the clothes that we wore the day before, but totally rested and for the first time that week, we actually felt relaxed. This was the first day that we had not awakened to an early alarm and a mission to complete since we left South Carolina. We surmised that our friends, family, and colleagues at home were envious of the romantic vacation they imagined we were on. If they only knew what we were actually doing – scaling buildings, breaking, and entering, and trying to help the police bust criminals.

We showered and got ourselves ready for our last day in Rome and the first actual day of our vacation. We had nothing planned and it felt great. It was going to be a day of enjoyment and hopefully a little bit of Italian entertainment. I asked Clare what she felt like doing.

Without hesitation, she said, "We have the entire day open. Why don't we travel up to Florence? I've always wanted to go there. We can visit the Sistine Chapel and see Michelangelo's David, and then we can rummage through the flea markets. They say you can get high-quality jewelry and leather at reasonable prices."

After what I had put Clare through the past few days, it sounded like a great idea. We would spend our last day doing whatever Clare wanted to do. Our GPS search told us Florence was about a three-hour drive. Six hours of travel time would give us about four to five hours to visit the sites. We went downstairs, ordered a coffee and pastry to go, summoned the valet, and before we knew it we were on the road. We had all day, and what happens, would happen. We were going to be tourists and just go with the flow.

Even though the traffic leaving Rome was heavy and there was some tricky maneuvering to be done, our sense of tranquility could not be shaken. Once we were out of the city we seemed to sail effortlessly to Florence. We drove through the Tuscan region with its rolling hills and cypress trees. Stone, wood, tile, and wrought iron clad homes dotted the landscape. The scene looked like an artist's painting that had come to life. We sat in silence except for the rock and roll classics that came from Clare's iPhone. This was heaven. I was wishing that we had more days to spend this way and wondered if we had wasted our time in Italy pursuing the markings at the Pantheon.

My mind wandered as it often does, to a book that I had just finished reading about trees and vegetation.

I turned to Clare and asked, "Did you know that trees can communicate with each other?"

Disinterested, she answered, "I can honestly say that I have never given it a moment of thought."

Undeterred, I continued to ramble, "They have communication links via their roots and they can alert one another of certain types of diseases that could befall them. They can even clone themselves. That's how forests grow naturally. Large stands of trees can modulate temperature and soak up carbon dioxide. That is, except for palm trees. They are poor absorbers."

Not getting a response from Clare, I continued, "Fungus has a wide underground network of roots that travels for miles and plays a significant role in forestation. We tend to attribute life to animals, but trees and plants have their own forms of life."

She finally responded and said, "Either you have been spending too much time on the world wide web or you have been reading some obscure science fiction."

In my defense, I said, "There is probably a lot we don't know about nature that we should know before we destroy it."

In the quiet moments of our day, our minds wandered to divergent places. I was sometimes amazed that I could be so in sync with someone who was so totally different from myself.

We continued the balance of the drive pointing out scenery to one another and listening to Clare's music. Soon the countryside became a cityscape and we found ourselves once again looking for a parking spot. We eventually found one, but it meant that it would be quite a walk to our first stop, Ponte Vecchio. We strolled through the crowds looking at gold jewelry behind glass cases. We purchased a pair of earrings with a swirling cage design that Clare liked. After that, we bought gelato and made our way over to the river.

Our next stop would be Cattedrale di Santa Maria del Fiore. As we made our way to the cathedral, we entered the Piazza della Signoria. There in the corner stood a replica of Michelangelo's David. This is where the original David stood until it was moved indoors. We were amazed at the detail. We took snapshots and then continued on our venture. We passed high-end shops and stores. Gucci, Louis Vuitton, and Cartier had a prominent presence. They were nice to look at but were out of our price range. The currency we shopped with in those stores was fantasy.

We eventually entered the large piazza where the enormous black and white Cathedral stood. We spent about half an hour examining the architecture and memorializing it. Hunger was setting in and we grabbed a quick bite to eat before we set off for Michelangelo's David at the Galleria dell' Accademia. We were impressed with the depth of detail in the statue and how it appeared so very lifelike. After lingering longer than we should have, we realized that it was getting late in the day and we wanted to get back to Rome before nightfall. Three and a half hours later we were maneuvering our way through the streets of

Rome and arrived at our hotel unscathed. It had been such a wonderful, relaxing day. It was exactly the type of day that you would imagine spending in Italy. Unfortunately, it was our final day.

We handed the car off to the valet and headed up to our room. The day was not over yet and we did not want to waste whatever time we had left in Rome in our hotel room. However, we spent our final evening, it had to be brief so we could pack and get to sleep before our 8:00 a.m. flight the next day. We decided to visit the Catacombs of Callixtus in Rome. After a brief rest, we went downstairs, called for a taxi and we were on our way. Our driver spoke English and he seemed to enjoy sharing local folklore with us. He dropped us off at a beautiful green area of gardens, statues, and open spaces for reflection. We paid the admission fee and we were soon in the depths of the Catacombs. These were no ordinary tombs. They housed famous individuals as well as Popes. We made our way through cavernous tunnels with arched ceilings that were both immense and foreboding. Carved out grey stone housed the bodies of the deceased. The tour lasted about an hour. Once we were back at the surface, we quickly called for a cab and headed to our room where we packed and prepared for our early morning flight. We settled into bed, knowing that we would have an exhausting day ahead of us.

When the 4:30 a.m. alarm sounded, we jumped out of bed, showered, and checked to make sure that we had not forgotten anything. The end of our stay in Rome was about to begin. The valet brought the car around and we raced off to the airport. This time, traffic was exceptionally light and we seemed to be doing well in regard to time. Once we were at the airport, we returned our car to the rental area, checked-in, and got our boarding passes. We were finally able to slow down and have at bite to eat at the breakfast bar. Afterwards with our reading material in hand, we settled into chairs and began the wait to board our flight.

Rather than read, I found myself scrolling through my phone, continuing my search for any information that could solve the mystery of the Pantheon. I wondered if I should send the Roman Center for Archeology a copy of our findings and let them in on our discovery, but I realized that doing so could get us in a boat load of trouble. The first question they would ask is how we got the pictures. I decided that it was best to keep our findings to ourselves for now. It was possible that I could uncover some more data back at home. If all roads pointed to a dead end then I might consider giving the information to the Romans.

The loudspeaker announced our flight and we boarded the plane. Except for turbulence as we entered U.S. airspace, we had a comfortable flight back home. The rocky portion of the flight unnerved me as it always does. Clare instinctively knew that I was stressing and she reached over and grasped my hand. We always joke that I have to bring one extra pair of underwear on every flight just in case.

After touchdown, we retrieved our bags, but when we went through customs, the officer directed us to secondary inspection. I always go into panic mode when this happens and mentally go over everything that I packed. Could it be the drone that triggered the inspection? The customs officer put on a pair of latex gloves and asked for permission to go through our luggage before diligently and methodically rifling through our personal belongings. He unzipped each bag and carefully started to remove items. He rummaged around and pulled out the drone, the flashlight, and the file. He then took out the computer and swabbed the keys. The swab was then inserted in a machine and the computer was put back in the bag. He then inspected the drone. He put it back in its bag, nodded and told us to have a lovely day.

We repacked our clothes and headed to our car. Going through customs is always intimidating. I feel guilty even when there is nothing to feel guilty about. And then there is the fear factor. My mind always wanders to the could have factor. Could someone have planted illicit drugs or something illegal in my luggage to set me up for whatever reason? It was always a nerve-wracking experience but today my paranoia was in overdrive. Luckily, we made it through unscathed, just as we should have, and we were finally on our way home.

Chapter VIII
HOME AGAIN

It was midafternoon by the time we pulled into our driveway. The grass needed cutting, the flowers were wilted, and weeds had sprouted, but other than that, it appeared to be just like we left it. The funny thing about getting away from home is how wonderful it feels to return. After unpacking and changing into more comfortable clothes, we agreed that there was nothing more enticing in that moment than a home cooked meal. I slapped together a late lunch and we devoured it like we had not eaten in days. Nothing we consumed in Rome compared to the simple, culinary delight that I had prepared. It was so good to be home.

As Clare went about tidying up the kitchen, I went outside to tackle the neglected yard. It was a hot, hazy, overcast day. I watered the plants, cut the grass, pulled weeds, and topped up the bird feeder. At the far end of the yard, I noticed a deer gracefully move through the property. As nice as it was to be in Rome, I did not miss the concrete and the cacophony of the city. When I entered the house, Clare was already sitting on the couch in the sunroom with a book on her lap. I joined her and asked what she wanted for dinner.

She looked at me and said, "Whatever you feel like cooking. I'm done for the day. All I feel like doing is curling up, watching television, and getting a good, restful sleep."

The end result was that we ordered pizza. We threw our paper plates and cutlery in the garbage and cleanup was done within a minute. We snuggled into the sectional in the living room, turned on the television and started the search for something worthwhile to watch. A channel showing a panoramic view of Rome caught my attention.

We looked at one another and simultaneously screamed, "We've been there. We have to watch this."

The program was a documentary, with the narrator chronicling ancient times. He spoke of how aliens may have been a factor in the construction of the city's ancient structures. This was an angle that I had not considered. Fascinated, we watched with laser focused interest. He claimed that evidence exists proving that extraterrestrials once visited us. UFO experts went on to explain the theories and used actual examples to back up their claims. I have always been skeptical of UFO and extraterrestrial sightings. My mind functions on logic. We are millions of miles away from anything remotely inhabited. Why would travelers from a distant planet be able to find us if we could not do the same? It just did not make sense to me. We are one of the most technologically advanced countries in the world. If we could not envision a way to find life forms on other planets, what type of technology would it take for an extraterrestrial to visit us. More ominous, why would they be interested in what we are doing on Earth.

By the time the show ended, Clare had fallen asleep on the couch. Her legs were draped over my lap, and I was able to gently move them without waking her. What she was unaware of, was that this UFO angle had piqued my interest, and in my mind, I had already tied it to the markings at the Pantheon. I walked over to the desk, found a pen and a pad of paper, and I started scribbling down the information that was provided in the broadcast. Clare must have sensed that I had moved away from the couch, because before I knew it, she was at my side watching what I was doing.

I looked up and said, "Clare, there may be something to this. We are constantly sending people to the moon to look for other forms of life. Maybe this race of beings is far more advanced technologically than we are."

And then I took it a step further, and perhaps a step too far for Clare. I suggested that maybe the markings on the Pantheon are an alien dialect signaling to us earthlings that we are not alone. It was at this point that Clare said we have had a long day and we need to go to bed and sleep. She then added that hopefully when we wake up in the morning, our minds will be refreshed. It was her gentle yet firm way of telling me that I needed to let this go. I knew she was thinking that we had our fun, and we had an unbelievable adventure, but we are home now and it was time to get back to reality. We had been together for so long; her words were expressed without uttering a word. With that, I acquiesced, crawled into bed, and snuggled up to my north star.

The next morning arrived with sunshine and warmth. Well rested, we hopped out of bed, dressed in our running gear, and started on our daily three-mile run. We left the countryside that surrounded our home and headed to an urban development of paved and winding streets. It was more physically draining than usual because it had been over a week since our last jog, but we endured and made it home exhausted but otherwise unscathed. We showered, ate breakfast, and then watched our usual Sunday morning human interest shows. Afterwards, Clare curled up with her book and I sat myself down in front of the computer to research aliens and UFOs. I was still wrapped up in the previous night's show.

My search eventually took me to the History Channel website which is full of information regarding sightings by government agencies around the world, including NASA. Most sightings are unexplained or are given an unconfirmed benign explanation. Digging deeper, I found interesting information in relation to the 1950's Roswell case. I read articles about the struggle between the Government and the citizens who claimed to have seen or have encountered UFOs. One famous sighting was the Phoenix lights in March 1997. Another involved the

Space Shuttle in September 1991. The Freedom of Information Act had given the public access to government documents which highlighted potential evidence of unearthly beings. The one consistent fact in the documentation was that whatever these occurrences were, there were no signs of aggression by these unexplained objects.

As a developing world, more countries are progressing into space travel. Enormous amounts of money are spent trying to find evidence of life on other planets. Of course, it is also used for more practical reasons such as communication, surveillance, and defense, but to those of us that grew up in the Star Trek generation, we think primarily in terms of someone being out there. Which brings me to this point. Why would a much more advanced civilization not launch exploration missions of their own? Could these beings have already discovered what we are only pursuing at this time? Our missions are based on discovery not conquering. Perhaps their missions are the same.

I sat and thought about what connection UFOs and the Pantheon could have. In ancient times, unidentified flying objects may have been viewed as deities or angels from above. Living centuries ago in a time when advanced science and technology did not exist, it is understandable that unexplained objects in the sky could have been given religious context. There would not have been any other explanation available. These celestial objects would then become recorded as gods in ancient hieroglyphs. Today we have the luxury of instant photography and a cell phone in virtually every hand. While the majority of these sightings can be logically explained away, some are unexplainable. My afternoon of research led me to the sinister conclusion that we are likely not alone in this universe. I had convinced myself that aliens are a real possibility. Anyone that knows me would be shocked to hear me say this. For them this would be an alien concept.

However, that was all I needed to take my research to the next level. I still could not let go of the markings at the Pantheon. Why I was so intrigued by them was unexplainable. Our secret mission in Rome had proved to be fruitless, but this alien angle gave me another reason to pursue my search for an answer. I would now have to figure out how to determine if these markings were placed in the Pantheon by alien beings. In my mind, they had to be connected. I decided to expand my research to unexplained alphabets or languages discovered anywhere on this planet.

I started by keying in alien markings. The first thing that appeared was crop circles. Over the years these geometric shapes cut into fields have been debunked as the work of pranksters and copycats trying to convince the world that it is the work of aliens. I moved on and found that records of strange, unexplained markings exist throughout the world. The Nazca lines in the desert of Peru were large geoglyphs made in the soil. The book *Chariots of Fire* tried to convince us that these were left by aliens as beacons for their navigation. Modern science has determined that they were created by the Nazca tribe who lived sometime around 100 AD. Next, I searched Egyptian and Chinese records but did not find any useful results. My conclusion was that there were no similar markings anywhere on earth. Or at least, there were no documented markings that were similar. At this point I realized that I would have to resort to a more unorthodox type of research.

I decided to print the markings and post them on my board for a closer look. I could hear each sheet drop from the printer to the floor as I continued to fruitlessly search the web. When I retrieved the pages, I noticed that I had printed the images on transparencies rather than paper and threw them in the garbage. I quickly reloaded the printer and started the process once again. When they finished printing, I pinned them to the corkboard, hoping that seeing them in a grouping would provide a better explanation as to what they meant. When this did not help, I carefully looked at each sheet, inspecting the patterns. I rotated the images. I tried different combinations of groupings and rotations, and I even tried pinning them up at an angle to see if it would unlock their secrets. Every attempt I made produced absolutely no results. I was as dumbfounded when I finished as when I started. Frustrated and exhausted, I decided to call it quits for the day before Clare could come in and tell me to. She always seemed to know my limits better than I did.

I found her in the kitchen, and as I reached for a beer I said, "I can't make any sense of those marks. Maybe they don't mean anything. Do you think I am getting too obsessed with this?"

She looked at me and said dead seriously, "Look honey, I know you. You will not let this go until you solve it. But keep in mind that it is not going to save the world and it is not going to change our lives. You are obsessing when there is no need to. The explanation could be as simple as the artist was doodling. Maybe he just wanted to leave his mark on the creation. Maybe it was code to shoot Marcus Agrippa or Caesar. It could have been his way of giving the building contractor the middle finger. All I know is that I miss having my husband by my side. You are physically here, but mentally you are far away."

She read the situation correctly and I told her that I would try to be more present while making a mental note to look for unexplained markings at my construction sites. I settled in for the evening with a book and valiantly tried to relax, but despite my best efforts, my mind wandered to the markings. I had to stop thinking about it. Tomorrow I was back to work and my focus needed to be on the demands of the day.

Chapter IX
ANOTHER DAY, ANOTHER DOLLAR

Monday morning arrived and I was back to my routine. After running, a shave, a shower, toast, and coffee, I was out the door and headed back to work. Clare would not be far behind me. I liked to beat the morning rush hour traffic and be at the office before 7:00 a.m. to plan, get organized and catch up on any overnight breaking news on my computer. Mackenzie was already at her desk and engrossed in her work when I arrived. I stopped and we greeted one another.

She politely asked, "How was your trip? Clare must have loved it."

"It was fantastic and she was over the moon to finally visit Rome. It was some much-needed time away. The ancient buildings were breathtaking," I replied.

We went on to kibbitz about what it would have been like to manage a project in those times and how challenging it must have been. It would have been a colossal feat to construct and coordinate without the tools, equipment, software, phones, and easy accessibility to the site that we have today. Taking that into consideration, the techniques they used were ingenious for that era. It would have been a project just to assemble the equipment needed to build the structure. The manager had to be a visionary and a master of improvision to get the job done. It would have taken weeks to months just to build the lifting equipment. Then trying to hire, house, feed, and co-ordinate the labor force would have been a monumental task.

I then shifted gears and asked, "How did things go for you last week?"

"They went really well. I met with the owner and they agreed to approve the extras which made Marc happy and he delivered on his promise. Productivity seems to be improving. You are going to be pleasantly surprised with our performance. I am just now working on the reports," she said with utter confidence.

After letting her know how pleased I was with her management performance, I headed to my office. The desk was piled high with files and documents that needed my signature. I walked over to the blinds and opened them to let the morning sun in. Settling into my chair, I sorted through the documents on my desk and organized them in order of importance. I reviewed them, applied my signature, and put them in my out basket to hand deliver later in the day. Opening my day timer, I went over the tasks that needed to be accomplished that day. I then booted up my computer and started reading the messages in my inbox. I wondered if my crew knew about the e-mail hierarchy triage. The first e-mails to be opened are from the boss, second are the ones from other VIPs in order of importance, and finally the ones with the most interesting subject line. Since I am the boss, I started looking for correspondence from my clients. I noticed that the team was starting to filter in. As they passed my office, employees slipped in to chat and update me on their projects. By this time Rome and the Pantheon had been relegated to the back of my mind. My focus was once again on work. I had successfully acclimated back into my life.

At 9:00 a.m. I headed to the boardroom for a general review meeting. This is where I get all the project managers together and they fill me in on the past two weeks' events and the next two weeks' game plan. We assess the progress of each project by highlighting the schedule, the cost, the productivity, and priority events. The meeting usually lasts about an hour with me acting as both the chair and the scribe. This way I can direct the course of the meeting and record it in such a way that it becomes the to do list for the next meeting. After business was completed and the staff disbursed, I returned to my office and typed up the minutes and e-mailed them to all interested parties. I then continued to respond to my e-mails. Since I was away for a week it took me more time than usual to get through the backlog. Afterward, I moved on to the customer relations portion of my job. I checked in with each executive level client to see if there were any pressing issues that needed my attention. Today our conversations started with my trip to Italy, then drifted to sports and finally to business. No one wanted to rip my head off today. Mackenzie seemed to have done an excellent job holding things together while I was gone.

Noon arrived quickly and I headed out of the office for a lunch meeting with the head of the local construction association whom I have known for at least ten years. The plan was to discuss changes to the way information and news is provided to its members. I would not be the only person convening with him today. Other contractors would be attending to provide their prospective and input. With all the current changes to safety regulations, I thought it would be prudent to develop a program that gives all contractors a simple outline of the changes and how it would affect them and the particular services they provide. The meeting lasted just over an hour with the president reviewing the options that the various service providers gave him. It ended with his assurance that he would discuss it with his team and get back to us. Lunch was over and we parted with the obligatory friendly handshake.

Back at the office, my afternoon was filled with more administrative work. I reviewed our profit and loss statement with the accountant. I asked him if our income could support a promotion and pay hike for one of our relatively new hires. Justin was hired ten months ago. He is an intelligent, hardworking employee, and fits well into the organization. Historically, it was at this point that we would lose an excellent employee to another company that was willing to pay more. My hope was that a pay increase and more responsibility would make him want to stay with our team. I did not want to lose him. Afterwards, I returned to my office. The barrage of meetings, emails and catch-up work seemed to be taken care of. No one needed my attention, and I found my mind wandering back to the markings in Rome.

Honestly, I was starting to doubt my own sanity. Clare was right. The markings were becoming my primary interest in life. My passion was the Pantheon, and everything else in my life had become obstacles keeping me from pursuing it. Maybe it was time to let it go. We had impulsively travelled to a foreign country and risked our freedom and our safety to find the significance of random marks etched into concrete. We came up empty handed and maybe that is what was meant to be. We added excitement to our predictable lives and we now had a story that we could only share with one another. It would be too dangerous to tell anyone else not only because of possible repercussions but because no one would believe us. Maybe I should be grateful that I have a wife that was open to pursuing this and let me have my fun. Maybe it was time to put it all to bed and get on with our lives.

In my mind, the rationale made perfect sense, unfortunately, that is not what I did. I started to search the internet for anything that might decipher what I was convinced was a code. Despite my efforts, I found absolutely nothing that would crack the mystery of the Pantheon. Next, I researched UFO experts and read their work and their theories. Some of the theories were a bit out there but others made sense. The one common thread was that they all felt that someone or something is out there and we are being watched. One even claimed that aliens walked among us by taking on the form of human beings. By doing so, they are able to infiltrate world governments with the goal of taking over the global command. My research was getting a bit creepy. I logged out of the science fiction, quickly checked my stock portfolio, and returned to the reality of my mundane business life.

Next on the agenda was a meeting with our chief estimator to go over a big proposal to manage the construction of a new fuel cell manufacturing plant. In the boardroom, Steve laid out the drawings, the specifications, and the estimate that he put together. We reviewed his presentation and went on to discuss the timeframe and the staffing needs the project would require. We concluded that we had enough people to staff the project and that the charge out rates would cover our expenses and leave us with a profit big enough to make it all worthwhile. I was already thinking about who I would assign to the project. It would be one of our biggest bids to date and I wanted to make sure I appointed the most competent and experienced manager to oversee it.

I asked him when the bid closes and if it was an electronic bid or did it need to be delivered. He told me that it closes the following day at 2:00 p.m. He went on to say that it is electronic but we have forty-eight hours to drop off the original signed breakdown. I felt good about this one. If we were successful, it would keep us busy for at least eighteen months.

"Nice work Steve. If we get this job, we might have to add to our workforce," I said as he bundled the documents.

By the time I returned to my office, it was 5:00 p.m. and the staff were already starting to wander out of the building. A welcome quiet was starting to envelope the office. I opened my day timer, scratched off my completed tasks and started a new list for the following day. After firing off more e-mails, I slammed my computer shut, turned the light off and walked out the door. Another day was done and I was once again headed home.

I was barely in the house when Clare asked me to come into the office. The sound of her voice told me something was up and I was a bit alarmed. She handed me the transparent plastic sheets of the markings that I had thrown in the garbage and said nothing.

Puzzled, I looked at her and said, "You have to give me a clue. I don't understand what the problem is. I accidently printed them on the wrong paper, so I threw them out and reprinted them."

She had a strange look on her face and her voice sounded frantic as she ordered, "Look at them! Can you see what you did?"

I was baffled. It was not like Clare to be stressed because I wasted paper. I obliged and looked at them once again but I still could not see the significance. She then told me to take a good long look. It was at this point that I saw it. When the sheets were superimposed on one another, it revealed some interesting features.

Incredulous, I asked, "How did you figure this out?

She explained, "It caught my eye when I was emptying the garbage can. With the sheets piled on top of one another, it looked like a single image. I played with them until these different shapes appeared."

"We may finally be onto something. We might have to try different combinations to figure it out, but this is a good start," I replied, impressed with her breakthrough findings.

Clare had prepared supper, so our focus shifted to filling our stomachs. A glass of wine and tasty food should clear our minds. Unfortunately, once we finished sharing our workday with one another, our conversation wandered to our latest discovery.

I looked at her and said, "I'm just going to throw this out there. I don't want you to think that I have lost my mind, but do you think the markings could be a message from unearthly beings?"

Clare, being the ever logical and pragmatic person that she is, smiled and said, "It's possible, but if it is, how would we ever decipher the message? I lost my decoder ring when I was five years old."

When I suggested that we build a bunker and hire a team of decoders, she laughed and said she may have to stage an intervention to keep me away from the History Channel. As we finished our wine we continued to good naturedly banter back and forth. Clare has always been witty and quick on her feet. In that department, I was really no match for her. While we were cleaning up the dinner dishes, I suggested that we stack the images in the same order that they appeared in the Pantheon. I could see that Clare was enthused with my idea. She ushered me into the office and told me to open the file with the drone video from the Pantheon while she leafed through the days mail.

Soon we were both sitting at the computer, excited about her discovery. We panned across each shot and we meticulously laid the sheets down one by one in the same order. The result was clearly an image of significance. But what the significance of the image was, remained a mystery. I stapled the sheets together and pinned them to the corkboard. There was definitely a pattern of dots, dashes, lines, and markings that were random and did not resemble anything familiar to us. I recalled that during a previous search there were undeciphered markings called Rongorongo scripts discovered on the Easter Islands. There were also Indus scripts found in Pakistan. I searched the websites once again and found that the Pantheon markings had similar characteristics. This could be a breakthrough. Theoretically this might connect different civilizations through a common denominator. Could the similar factor be aliens?

I turned to Clare and said, "I know there is something here but I just don't know what it is. I'm going to share this with my friends that are better educated in history and the arts than I am. I'll make up a story that we found the drawings in an old book and see what they make of it."

We printed up another set for Clare and stapled it together in the same order. She said she would share it with a friend that was an art major. It was now 10 :00 p.m. and time to put ourselves and the mystery of the Pantheon to bed for the night.

Making my way to work the next morning, I was once again consumed with the markings. This time, however, I was thinking about who I would approach to take a look at the transparencies and what plausible reason I could give for my interest that would not garner suspicion. I decided to approach three colleagues that I also considered friends. At the top of my list was David. He was a brilliant engineer and a graduate of Harvard with both an MBA in mechanical engineering and a PHD in engineering. We met years ago at a fabrication plant outside of Buffalo when we were just starting out. I was a contract coordinator and David was our chief design engineer. In my eyes, David is a genius. We had collaborated on an algorithm that we were able to copyright. I had asked him if he could derive a formula that would convert raw data like labor hours or time into a bell or S curve. David was never one to turn down a challenge and in little more than a week he developed a handy little program that did exactly what I envisioned. He was definitely first on my list. I decided on two other close friends. Lev was a wizard at financial affairs and Sam excelled in science. My cousin Logan, an archeologist, was also on the list.

The morning raced by as it usually does with emails, calls, and meetings. Before you could blink an eye, it was lunchtime and I could take a breather from work matters and shift my focus to my passion project. I called David, who is now the owner of his own engineering company. We had stayed in touch both personally and professionally over the years, so it would not seem out of the ordinary for him to hear from me or for me to ask him for a hand with something. After the obligatory salutations and catching up on one another's family, I told him about the drawings. I did not tell him the truth about where I found the original or how I obtained the rest of the drawings in the set. Rather, I told him that I had discovered them in an old book and they had captured my imagination.

He laughed and said, "I see that you are going down another wormhole."

David said he would be happy to give his opinion. He said it had been too long since we had gotten together and suggested that we meet for lunch the next day. That worked for me, and we agreed on a time and location. And just like that, my number one referral was locked in. I could always count on David and I was hoping that he would come through for me.

I followed up with calls to Lev and Sam. They were both happy to oblige and we set up a time to meet. Finally, I called my cousin Logan who was intrigued but had too many questions about where I found the symbols and why I was so interested in them. Once he was done interrogating me, he said he would be happy to help and we made plans to meet the following week. The rest of the day wound down quickly and I found myself arriving home earlier than usual. Clare was just walking up the sidewalk when I pulled in the driveway. She was surprised to see me.

"This never happens. Dinner is usually ready by the time you get home. Did they kick you out?" she asked in a joking manner.

She did not wait for my answer and went on to tell me that she showed the transparencies to an associate at work who was a major history buff. She learned that he was also familiar with ancient alien theories. This guy seemed like a perfect fit. She showed him the copies and he agreed to do some research for us. He told Clare that he would get back to her after he referred to his files and books.

I misunderstood her and asked, "Did you give him a copy?"

She assured me that she only showed it to him. She did not want it passed from hand to hand until we had established what it actually was.

The next day I arrived at the restaurant where David and I had planned to meet. When I entered, I saw him sitting alone at a table with his cell phone at his ear. When he noticed me, he ended the call. After we exchanged pleasantries and a handshake, we caught up on family and work. We shared our predictable gripes about the business we were in and concluded that it was not the love of the job that kept us going. It was the love of the money it provided us and the comfortable lives that we were able to provide our families. The money was like a drug. The more we got, the more we wanted.

Eventually, we moved on to what I really came to discuss. I told him about the bizarre markings that we had found, but I altered the story. I told him that they were found in an old book that we bought at an obscure bookstore. He asked to see them and I handed him the transparencies. He gazed at them intently. Slowly he flipped through each one and mumbled that the photos were amazing. His first guess was that it was a secret code to the location of ancient treasures left behind by a lost civilization somewhere in the Middle East. He told me to take the prints and place them on a glass mirror and then box it in on all four sides with mirrors. He said if I placed a lit candle in each corner and peered through red glazed glass down at the markings, I would find the location of the treasure.

He went on to say, "I think you may have just made a major discovery."

When I asked him how he knew, he told me that he has come across ancient literature that depicted these markings. I looked at him in stunned silence.

He stared back at me intently and said, "Jim, I'm bullshitting you. I don't have any idea what the hell these things are."

He started laughing and asked why I am so interested in this stuff.

Feeling somewhat offended, I replied, "You know me. When I find something that is unusual, I can't let it go."

Still smiling, he said, "Remember the pictures you took in California that you thought showed a scrapped Boeing B314? It was just a picture of a movie prop."

He said he could not help me with my quest, but I was welcome to pay for lunch. He did offer to see if he could find any information regarding the pictures. We finished our meals; I did pay the bill and we parted ways and headed back to work. It was nice to meet with David and catch up on one another's lives even if he thought my request was a joke.

Back at the office I returned a call from Sam. He told me that he had to reschedule our meeting because his son had a school play that he had forgotten about. We agreed to meet another time. After my lunch with David, I realized that if he had no idea what the markings were, it was quite likely no one else would either. I was beginning to think that this would become a dead file sitting in my desk drawer, untouched until my heirs found it after my death. They would find its significance and discover a cure for cancer or another worldly breakthrough. I knew it was time to file the pictures, erase them from my thoughts and return to life as we knew it.

That evening, I tried to decompress and accept the fact that this may be one of those things in life that just does not have any answers. The markings may have been nothing more than the artisan taking creative license and leaving his lasting imprint on what could be a structure that endures through the ages. Maybe he had a quirky sense of humor. I told Clare about how David played me at lunch and got me going with his crazy story about a lost ancient treasure. I left feeling ridiculed by someone I respected. Although I was ready to give up, Clare was not about to accept defeat. She felt that if we continued searching, we might stumble onto something.

She repeated the mantra that she had quoted repeatedly throughout the years we had shared together, "Failure is just a step towards success."

I told her that it is difficult to view every setback that we encountered as a move forward, and that it is difficult to envision success when all we encounter is failure.

In true Clare fashion, she looked me squarely in the eye and said, "That is when perseverance and plain old grit comes into play. If you give up whenever things get tough, you will never succeed. What we have experienced is not failure, it is success not yet achieved."

Once again, my wise partner set me straight. She went on to say that there is a fine line between ardently pursuing something and becoming obsessive in the search. We had a good life, a good family, and good jobs. To define the success of our lives by being able to decipher an obscure marking is losing perspective. She said our search for an answer should be a part of our lives, but we had to keep in mind that the search is not our reason for existing. If in the end we came up empty, that would be all right. When she said we had to keep things in perspective, I knew she was really saying I needed to regroup and reign myself in. She was right but whether I could follow through remained to be seen.

Chapter X
NEW DISCOVERIES

After a few relatively quiet days at the office, all hell broke loose. One of our industrial projects was shut down due to a fire that started in a pharmaceutical mixing room. When the call came in, I jumped in my car and rushed to the jobsite hoping we were not the cause. As I got closer to the massive facility, I felt a sense of relief. I did not see any smoke or fire rising above the plant. After being cleared at the security gate I made my way to our jobsite trailer. As I pulled in, I could see the flashing red and blue lights of fire trucks and police cars. Firemen suited up with air packs and masks were rolling out hoses. The plant personnel were evacuated and milling around outside in the parking lot. My site manager and his six-man crew were standing near the trailer. When I asked if we had done anything to cause the fire, to my relief, the manager said he did not think we were culpable. They had not been welding or doing anything that could spark a fire. Apparently, the crew were installing a small tank when the fire alarm went off and they were told to evacuate over the loudspeaker.

I tried calling and texting the plant manager to see if I could be of any assistance but had no success. Realizing that there was nothing that I could do at the site, I went back to work. That was a bit too much excitement for a Friday morning. Shortly after I returned to the office, the plant manager returned my call. Apparently, one of the mixer motors overheated and set a belt on fire. It caused a great deal of smoke before the sprinklers kicked in. He wanted me to know that he had asked my crew to do the repairs. They replaced the motor and the belt and got the plant up and running for the afternoon shift. He went on to praise my team and thanked me for the support.

Although I knew we had a competent crew at the site, I was also keenly aware that accidents could happen. Working in an operating facility has its challenges and has to be done with extreme care. Barriers must be put in place to keep us separated from the operations of the facility, and special health and safety rules apply in order to avoid injury. Each morning requires a crew briefing as to what work is approved for the day and in what areas we are allowed to work. Activities such as welding require permits and a fire watch to ensure that safeguards are in place. Whenever something goes wrong, there is always that initial sense of panic that someone in my crew cut corners or slacked off on safety protocols.

We experienced an almost disastrous fire at a paper mill project on a previous job. Our welder was attaching a bracket to a column two levels up from the basement. All the safety procedures were reviewed and adhered to. What we failed to do was a thorough follow-up inspection on the lower levels. Our fire watch did not realize that there was a small gap between the column and the floor through which it was rising. During the welding operation, both the welder and the watch were wearing heavily tinted glasses to protect their eyes. The glass was so dark that a small bit of welding spark that was almost undetectable, fell through the gap to the lower level. Since the plant was operational, there was dried wood pulp residue in small nooks and crannies throughout the plant. This tiny spark found its way down to the basement level and lodged itself into a dried-up clump of pulp. It must have smoldered for quite a while. After the day shift left, the night crew arrived to find a blazing inferno in the basement. Fortunately, it was contained and there was relatively minor damage to any other part of the facility. That forced us to revise our fire watch procedure and increase the inspection area after welding operations. We also implemented a fire watch delay clause that requires the individual to stay at the location a full half hour after the welding was done as a precaution.

The rest of the day passed crisis free and I did something that I rarely do. I packed up early and headed home, hoping to plan a possible trip to the mountains with Clare. After our action packed, stressful trip to Rome, a quiet time in the mountains seemed like the perfect vacation to recover from our previous vacation. It would be a time we could enjoy nature and one another. When I pulled into the garage, I noticed that Clare was not home yet. The first thing I did when I entered the house was reach in the fridge and crack open an ice-cold beer. I went out back and sat at the patio table watching the birds darting back and forth to the bird feeder that I had suspended midair from a wire rope. This was one of those rare times that I sat in absolute silence, not thinking about what had passed and not worrying about what the future may bring.

Within minutes I noticed a squirrel eyeing the feeder. It stared intently at the wire rope strung between the two trees that supported it. After a minute or two of quiet reflection, it sprang into action. It scaled the tree trunk and made its way up to where the wire attached to the tree. The squirrel's shenanigans captivated me. The morning's fire and the day's demands were now far behind me. All that mattered in that singular moment was what the squirrel would do next. To my amazement, he scaled his way over to the feeder hanging upside down, moving claw after claw for support. Once he was positioned directly above it, he made his way down to the feeder and started eating the sunflower seeds, paying no attention to the nearby birds darting to and from the feeder. It then jumped to the ground and without any hint of injury, he sped away. This was a better show than the flying Wallendas. I relished the sense of peace and utterly satisfying calm that I have rarely felt in my life. This must be what they refer to as being at one with the world. In this moment all the work-related stresses, any family related worries, and the mystery of the markings had just melted away and exited my body. I finally understood what it felt like to be in a state of total relaxation and I owed it to some birds and a wily squirrel. I shut my eyes, tilted my face to the sun and savored the warm air and the cool breeze on my face.

Soon I could hear the garage door opening. Clare was home and all was right with the world. After finding me out back and making sure that nothing was wrong, she said she was going to go inside, change and pour a glass of wine. Within minutes she was back outside with her drink and another beer for me. She did as she always does and gave me a rundown of her day.

She sat down across from me, sighed, and started by saying, "What a week this has been. I got extraordinarily little done. It was one meeting after another. One of the meetings devolved into group therapy rather than troubleshooting or problem solving. Between the drama queens and the grandstanders, it was like an audition for a horror movie. Thank god for Pinot Noir."

We raised our drinks and toasted to a good weekend. She was amazed by how mellow I seemed. She even comically checked my pulse to make sure that I was still alive. She said she did not understand what had come over me, but whatever it was, she loved it. She could not remember seeing me so Zen. Jokingly, I told her that one of her chef's special T-bones and some more brew could make me even more Zen. She laughed and said she would get the steaks ready for the barbeque, but the grilling was still my job.

While we were eating, Clare told me that she had information about the symbols. The guy at work thought they could be some kind of communication device to connect with aliens. To me, it sounded like she had a friend that was getting a kick out of toying with her.

I looked at her and said, "Come on Clare. He's just messing with your head."

She replied, a bit defensively and said, "I don't think so. He's not that type of guy. He was dead serious. He said we have to go where the symbols are located and shine a light underneath them and towards the sky. That would capture the attention of the aliens."

Skeptically, I replied, "Clare, he is messing with you. It is way too science fiction to be real. I wish you had spoken to him before we went to Rome. We could have debunked his theory while we were there."

I could not believe that my intelligent wife was buying into this guy's nonsense. What she said next sounded even crazier. She said this friend believes that there is a gateway to an alien transponder where the markings originated. She was utterly serious and I was trying not to laugh. We were not at all in agreement on this. This was not my Clare. I was starting to think that an alien had abducted her and was posing as my wife. She had utmost trust and faith in this colleague, and I thought he was an order of fries short of a happy meal.

Still on the defensive, she said, "He is a very smart and competent fellow. I have known him for five years and he would not jerk me around. I respect his work ethic and his capabilities. Just because he believes in aliens does not mean that he is irrational. What he suggested is not crazier than the two of us going to Rome, scaling, and breaking into an ancient building to get pictures of scribbles that we noticed on your father's home movie."

My usually even-tempered wife was getting animated and I could tell that she honestly believed what this guy told her. It was not like her to be reckless. Between the two of us she was the wise, steady partner. Most often it was me running off on tangents and wild goose chases. In that moment, I knew by her demeanor that it was time to just listen because she was obviously taking his words seriously.

She then reminded me and said, "Even you are starting to believe in life on other planets that may be far more advanced than we are."

Clare pointed to all the sightings I had researched since we returned from Rome. She said she did not want to be a UFO chaser and start going to Star Trek conventions, but she did think there may be something out there. She suggested that we just keep open minds and see what transpires. With a lame stab at humor, I accused her of wanting to go back to Rome.

At that point she replied with a big smile and said, "We didn't really get to see Tuscany."

We both laughed. I do not know if it was the alcohol kicking in or my utter state of relaxation, but it did sound like a promising idea. We knew that we could not just pack up and leave for Rome so soon after returning. We both had responsibilities and obligations at home. The summer weather in Rome would be stifling, so we decided to put it on our calendars for the fall and hope that we could actually make it there.

We went in the house intending to turn in for the night, but her friend's theory had me intrigued. Now this should have been the end of an amazing, relaxing evening but it was not. I had morphed back to what was now my normal state of being. I told Clare that I wanted to go out back, try out her friend's theory and see if anything happened. Without hesitation, she joined me. My partner in crime and I were back on the same page again. I retrieved the transparencies from the office and then went to the garage where I found a powerful spotlight and a ridiculously long extension cord. Next, I went in the house and came out with our glass side table. This would support the transparencies and allow room for the spotlight underneath. Once we had things in place, I switched on the spotlight and we both looked to the skies. We did not see anything out of the ordinary.

We switched the light off and brainstormed. We decided to add color, hoping that we would get a different result. Being both a handyman and a hoarder it should not be difficult finding something in my overstuffed garage. I rummaged through accumulated parts, scraps and pieces of various materials and found a box with plastic sheets of assorted colors. I grabbed pieces of red, green, and blue and ran back to the yard. My adrenaline was once again pumping. My state of Zen from earlier in the evening was now a distant memory. We first placed the green sheet of plastic on the table and then the blue. Both times, nothing happened. Finally we placed the red sheet on the table and once again, there was nothing unusual in the sky.

Just as I was about to pull the red sheet off the table, Clare yelled, "Look!"

I looked up to the skies and there was a small red dot of light appearing to descend rapidly to earth, then stop and change its color to blue before firing away into the night sky. It was like a shooting star without a tail and it was able to make a ninety-degree turn. We were both jumping out of our skin. If any of our neighbors saw us, they would have thought that we were either utterly intoxicated or just simply insane. There was no music, no nothing. Just two crazy people having the time of their lives for no apparent reason.

I screamed to Clare, "Holy crap! What the hell was that? Did we really see that or did we just psych ourselves into believing that we saw it?"

We tried doing it again but nothing happened. We decided that whatever was in the sky, recognized that we were not at the right location. Her friend did say that we had to be at the exact spot where we found the markings.

After putting all the paraphernalia away, we sat down in the kitchen and tried to make sense of it. We even toyed with the idea of immediately heading back to Rome. So much for being sensible and responsible adults.

I looked at Clare and asked, "If we have found a signal to the aliens, do you know what that means? This could be a world-shattering discovery. We would either become celebrated heroes in the history books or certified lunatics and a threat to national security. They might ship us off to Sing-Sing and I would become someone's bitch."

We were once again laughing. The levity was helping. We agreed that we had to go to Rome sooner than the fall and decided on the following month. This would give us time to prepare and figure out how we were going to get the set-up accomplished at the Pantheon. We decided that our best option was to order whatever material we needed through Amazon and have it delivered to Italy. We still could not believe what we had just seen, but what we saw, turned both of us into true believers.

Clare left the room and turned on the computer in the office. In no time, she had booked our flights, our hotel, and a vehicle. This was really going to happen. We cracked open a bottle of Prosecco and toasted to our sighting and our next adventure. Who knew that an old home movie would set a couple of baby boomers on a course of mystery and intrigue? We joked about hiring a film crew to follow us around and document it for the History Channel. We would become famous and have a circle of little green men for friends. We burst into laughter. What a crazy day it had been. My day started in horror at the scene of a fire that my crew could have been responsible for and progressed to sitting in utter tranquility in my backyard being entertained by birds and squirrels. Now I was having trouble containing myself thinking that I had just witnessed a possible UFO sighting, and soon we would once again be on our way to Rome.

Tapped out, we headed upstairs to bed. Still feeling playful, I winked at Clare and said, "Since we are heading into the twilight zone, I think I can find a way to send you to the moon tonight."

Clare answered in her best Mae West impression, "Well look at you Mr. Spaceman. Is that a rocket that I see you are launching? Houston, it looks like we don't have a problem. All systems are a go."

And that is how the night ended with a bang.

Chapter XI
HOLDING PATTERN

The next four weeks plodded along at a mercilessly slow pace. We tried to contain our anticipation by deliberately shifting our focus to work and other routine aspects of our lives. On weekends, we had our grandson over for a couple of sleepovers. Time spent with him always transported us to an alternate world of parks, splash pads, dance parties and movie nights. Clare would bake and paint with him. I would take him on walks through the woods and search for flowers, birds, squirrels and potentially any other exotic animal that may lurk among the trees and shrubbery. One night, when we were looking at the constellations, my grandson swore that he saw a UFO. In a very grandfatherly way, I told him there was no such thing as extraterrestrials and that it must have been a shooting star. I flat out lied to him so he would not frighten himself. If he knew that his Nana and Papa had become true believers in aliens and unidentified flying objects he would never again get a good night's sleep.

We made a point not to skip our morning runs. Our mental health depended on it. We would suit up in our athletic gear, grab a water bottle and drive to various trails. Clare was more of an avid runner than I was, and she would motivate me to keep up with her. Our running style was slow and steady. Despite the pace, most days I still failed to keep up with Clare. When I went out on my own, I would often just walk.

Our favorite trail was about twenty minutes away and it took us along country roads, past grazing cattle, dilapidated homesteads with weathered grey wood siding, crumbling chimneys, and rusted tin metal roofs. Through the overgrown brush, you could see leaning structures that we imagined would have housed small families hundreds of years ago. Old, abandoned farm implements dotted the yards, barely visible through the overgrowth. Trying to visualize life in those rustic times fascinated me. Over the years, I had read various preserved diaries of the homesteaders. Life was difficult in those days, and medicine was scarce. Sometimes the treatment for an ailment was worse than the disease. People died never knowing what was killing them.

The trail was pretty quiet most days. Part of the run is along a river. On sunny days, the rays of sunlight would glisten and bounce off the water as it peaked through the tree branches. Flocks of ducks floated on the water as if they did not have a care in the world. Canada geese waddled along the riverbank, seeming to coexist in harmony with the ducks. Every now and then, they would startle us as they squawked and took to the air. Not everyone was a runner on the trail. Nature lovers would sit on intermittent benches absorbing the beauty of the nature preserve. Most days we ran for a mile and a half and then turned around and made our way back to the car for the drive home. Our morning run is the most physically demanding activity of the day, and yet it is usually the most relaxing part of the day.

We also tried to connect with friends and neighbors. That evening we were scheduled to visit a couple who lived a ten-minute walk up the road. Madison and John Hill are neighbors that we met when we moved into the area. Madison is a dental hygienist and John is a consultant in the power transmission field. They are from Alaska and have never lost their love for the wilderness. Their pioneering spirit is reflected in the rustic home they built fifteen years ago. Entering their house is like walking into an old hunting lodge. The great room has soaring ceilings, wood clad walls and a massive field stone fireplace. Old, framed pictures hang on the walls and the room is furnished with overstuffed wood framed couches covered in down filled cushions.

They had prepared an eclectic meal of balsamic infused vegetables and meats, paired with Cabernet. Dinner conversation centered on our trip to Italy and their recent trip to Alaska. I admired how they sought out remote, off the grid locations to visit. The evening passed quickly. I do not know if it was the heat coming from the fireplace or the excessive amount of food and good wine, but something was starting to make me drowsy. That was our cue to bid our host farewell. After hugs and a thank you we walked home in the darkness of the night, the silence only broken by the occasional hoot of an owl and the sound of the crunching twigs that we stepped on. The darkness had engulfed us and left us feeling isolated from the world. Other than the two of us, there seemed to be no other signs of human life.

Once we were home, we sat outside on the patio, gazing up at the star-studded sky, spotting and naming the constellations. Occasionally we would see the twinkling lights of a plane passing through, taking its passengers to what we imagined was a far-off exotic destination. There was a half crescent moon that shed its white glow onto the trees and lawn. We sat for quite a while just soaking in the beauty of the night before getting up and heading to bed.

Chapter XII
WELCOME BACK

The month of waiting was ending and we were days away from our much-anticipated return to Rome. We were starting to pack and with every item added to our suitcases, our excitement escalated. We had already bought black tights, long sleeved black shirts, balaclavas, and black gloves for our clandestine operation. Friends and family were telling us how jealous they were that we could once again pack up and fly back to Rome. We played along with them and led them to believe that one week in Rome was not enough. We were empty nesters with established careers, and we were finally going to take advantage of the fruits of our years of labor. If they knew what we were really going for, they would have locked us up, ordered a psychiatric evaluation, and prevented us from boarding the plane. Little did they know and little did we want them to know.

We were flying business class this time and were looking forward to enjoying the perks that came with it. You only live once, and Clare decided that we deserved the better food, wine and real plates and cutlery that came with the upgrade. We ate, drank, and relaxed in the extra-large, extra comfortable seats. When the lights dimmed, we were both able to fall asleep without difficulty. When we opened our eyes, we were circling over Rome. I could see the Colosseum and the ancient ruins knowing that we would soon be walking among them.

When the plane landed, we grabbed our luggage, cleared customs, and picked up our rental vehicle. Once again, we found ourselves in a Fiat. This time it did not seem as foreign to us as we made our way back to the same hotel at which we had previously stayed. We checked in and found ourselves in a room with a somewhat classical contemporary design. We quickly unpacked and were ready to get down to business.

We turned on the computer and accessed the information highway. I could not help but think what slaves we have become to the massive amounts of information available at the touch of a button, the advertisements ready to sell us anything imaginable, in addition to having our personal stored data available at any time. Losing our luggage would have been a problem. Losing our laptop or our phone would have been catastrophic. I thought about how these pieces of machinery that have the ability to spy on us, have enslaved us. The privacy that was lost was outweighed by the easy access of information.

I needed to order a compact spotlight and a small folding glass table to hold the transparencies that we had brought to Italy with us. With one click, the items were ordered, paid for, and guaranteed to arrive the next day. Amazing. Clare was sitting on the bed leafing through pamphlets and magazines advertising the area. She was looking for a place to eat. I suggested that we should first go to the Pantheon and figure out how we were going to get inside after hours.

"Sounds good," she said. "We can have an amazing meal afterwards. This could be our last supper before we are arrested for break and enter."

I was not sure that she was kidding about the break and enter even though she said it in a playful manner. She was far more apprehensive than I was, but even so, she seemed eager to conduct our mission. We were a team, but I knew that Clare had a tipping point.

We made the same, now familiar walk to the Pantheon that we had taken on our previous trip. Once we were in the piazza we penetrated the crowd and worked our way to the portico through the massive bronze doors. Once we were inside, we made a right turn and followed the interior wall looking for a place to conceal ourselves. We did not notice any bathrooms that we could hide in, so we had to get creative about how we could conceal ourselves after hours. Once we made a full three-sixty around the inside of the building, we realized that there really was no place to hide. The best that we could do was tuck ourselves behind one of the statues or under the grand alter. After closer examination, we realized that even if we dieted until we were skin and bones, we would still be unable to fit in the tight space behind the statues. We decided that our hiding spot would have to be somewhere under the alter. We started to look for motion sensors and cameras. All the cameras above the main alter seemed to be pointing towards the entrance.

There was nothing more to be done, so we decided to find someplace to eat lunch and return at closing time to see what procedure was followed to clear the building. We decided on the same outdoor café that we had dined at during our previous visit. We chowed down on pizza and sipped a carafe of Chianti as if we did not have a care in the world.

After some thought, I said to Clare, "I think what we have to do when we return at closing time is to blend in and mingle with the other tourists. We can watch to see how thorough a job they do clearing out the visitors without drawing attention to ourselves. To make our plan bullet proof we can create a diversion a few minutes before they usher everyone out. This would distract the security and give us a chance to get in position in our hiding spot."

We decided to buy a burner phone and set the alarm to go off right before closing. We would plant it near the front door and place it on a ledge so it looked like someone forgot it. By the time they figure out that it is a burner phone and no one will be coming forward to claim it, we would be settled in under the alter. After the building clears out we would be able to get to work. We decided that Clare would carry a large purse to house our materials. This would draw less suspicion than a backpack if someone were to review the security tapes. We decided to pick one up on our way back to the hotel. Our dark clothes would be hidden underneath our street attire. We were keenly aware that the cameras would be recording while we were trespassing in the building but we hoped they would not be reviewed unless there was some reason to do so.

The rest of our afternoon was unplanned. This gave us time to wander the cobblestone streets of the city and marvel at the architecture. We walked past the Spanish stairs and then moved onto the Jewish ghetto and past the Trevi Fountain. It felt like we were tourists, except we knew that we were not. Ten minutes before closing, we returned to the Pantheon. Our timing proved to be perfect. We once again entered the awe-inspiring building and mingled with other tourists pretending to admire the works of art. Within minutes, security personnel were herding up the tourists motioning them to move towards the door. We moved with the crowd as it squeezed into the portico and out to the piazza. I stopped at the door and looked back to see if the guards were sweeping the interior looking for people that could be hiding in the building. It did not seem to be a part of their closing routine.

We returned to our room and got ready for the exclusive dinner that we had planned. Dressed in evening wear, we made our way to Cucina de Momma. After an exquisite meal, we finished our wine and made our way back to our room. Exhausted and having accomplished our goal for the day, we laid down on the bed, and turned on the television. The next thing we knew, it was morning.

We awoke fully rested and decided to go for a run through the narrow streets, up and down the alleyways, and past the ruins. After a two-mile run and a warm shower, we headed to the café for breakfast. When we returned to the room, we noticed that the little red light on the room's landline was flashing. I called the front desk and was told that my package had arrived. After retrieving it, I ripped the box open to find my much-anticipated battery powered spotlight, spare batteries and a small ten by ten steel framed glass table with folding legs. I wasted no time and set the table up, placed the piece of red plastic that we had brought with us on top and positioned the spotlight under it. Rays of red light shined through the glass onto the ceiling above.

Now that I had the equipment, I remembered that I still needed to buy the burner phone. Clare was sitting in the corner chair reading. I told her that I would run out and pick one up. I headed up the street toward a nearby shop that I had noticed earlier in the day. Once inside, I made my way up and down the rows of gadgets and trinkets until I finally found the phones. I settled on a compact grey phone with an alarm function. When I took it to the counter, I asked the clerk if I could check the alarm for volume. He was agreeable and grabbed a pack of batteries off the counter, ripped the packet open and inserted them in the phone. The screen lit up and I quickly moved myself through the few functions that the phone was equipped with. I set the alarm to go off in one minute. Just as expected, the phone put out a faint rhythmic sound that I was able to increase with the volume control. I paid for the phone and batteries and left the store.

On my way back to the room, the smell of fresh baked bread led me to a bakery where I picked up sweets and a loaf of warm crusty bread to share with Clare. Not only do I have a sweet tooth, but I also cannot resist a loaf of fresh baked bread. On my way back to the room, I tore off a piece and shoved the warm, delectable wonder into my mouth. Unfortunately, one bite led to another and then another. When I reached the room, I handed the pastries and the mangled loaf to Clare.

She looked at the bread and asked sarcastically, "What happened here? Are they selling gently used bread at the bakeries today?"

I told her that I was attacked by a ferocious mob of mice and had to rip the pieces off to appease them and save my life. We shared a laugh before confessing that I just could not help myself. After our lighthearted banter, I showed her the phone that I had bought and demonstrated the ring volume. We now had everything we needed to accomplish our mission and we decided that we would go forward with our plan that night. If the conditions did not prove to be favorable, we would try again the next night. We made a final run through our plan and made contingency plans should anything go wrong. There was no room for error. We continued rehearsing until it was time to leave. We stuffed Clare's purse with the spotlight, glass, and transparencies and added the balaclavas and gloves as an afterthought. I placed the burner phone in my pocket and we left our personal cellphones in our luggage so we could not be tracked.

As the time to leave approached, we slipped into our black tights and t-shirts and pulled our street pants on top so we would not look like cat burglars. I glued a fake mustache above my upper lip and a pair of dark rimmed glasses concealed my eyes. A baseball cap finished the disguise. Clare put her hair in a bun and wore a wide brimmed straw hat. She laid her makeup on ridiculously thick and totally different from how she would normally apply it. After putting on our black sneakers, we looked at ourselves in the mirror. Not bad for a couple of amateur spies.

We left the hotel and within ten minutes we were standing in front of the Pantheon. I pulled the phone out of my pocket, turned it on, adjusted the volume and set the alarm for 7:10 p.m. We were relieved to be in the final stages of our plan and at the same time we were extremely anxious as we entered the building. Should just one thing go wrong and we were caught, it could totally change our lives.

We casually made our way into the grand building and saw that it was filled with tourists. The more people there were in the building, the less conspicuous we would be. We were off to a good start. It was not quite 7:00 p.m. and closing time was only fifteen minutes away. We scanned the area and found a hidden place to leave the phone. Casually, I walked up to the column and leaned on it, as if I was tired of waiting for someone. I took the phone out of my pocket, wiped it clean and set it on a ledge behind the column. No one seemed to notice and I could not see a nearby camera that would pick it up. I thought to myself that things were going just as we had planned. I joined Clare near the center of the building where we acted like typical tourists.

Careful never to look in the direction of the security camera, we slowly mingled our way to the front alter, marveling over its shape and size. Within minutes, we noticed the guards assemble as they prepared to shepherd the visitors towards the entrance doors. The alarm on the phone went off as scheduled, stopping people in their tracks. Startled tourists quickly and instinctively moved towards the door to escape potential danger. We moved into place behind the alter. The guards started shouting commands and moved swiftly towards the sound. Everyone seemed to be focused on the noise coming from the column. It could not have unfolded more perfectly.

Finally, a guard grabbed the phone and held it up in the air to show that it was just a phone.

He yelled out first in Italian and then in broken English, "Did anyone lose a phone?"

There was no response and he slipped it in his jacket pocket.

Meanwhile, we sat quietly and waited. We could hear the noise from the crowd dissipate as the room slowly emptied. We heard conversation amongst the guards that we could not understand, and then the massive bronze doors were closed. Next we could see the guards do a walk around the building, in what we assumed was a final scrub for stragglers. Within minutes, the lights were turned off and we could hear the clanking of keys as the doors were locked. Except for the two of us, the building was now eerily empty. We waited for about ten minutes to make sure there was no one left in the building or in case someone returned to retrieve something they had forgotten. We sat in dead silence not daring to move or even sneeze in the darkness. The only light in the room came through the oculus.

When we determined that we were safe, we crawled out from under the alter and looked around. The quiet was haunting. The sculptures and statues seemed to stare down on us as if in judgement of what we had done and what we were about to do. This must have been my conscience talking. Clare stood silently by my side not saying a word. She had a strained look on her face as we glanced at one another. We kept our talk to a whisper and spoke only if we were unable to communicate through hand jesters. We were keenly aware that there could be microphones in the building. Our outerwear was quickly removed. We were now in solid black attire. We added the black gloves and the balaclavas to complete our disguise. By being totally attired in black, we hoped that if we were caught on camera, we would look like shadows.

Next, we pulled the spotlight, the glass table, and the transparencies from Clare's purse and we filled the bag with the clothing that we had removed. We then stuffed the purse under the alter to conceal it. Silently, we stepped down and moved towards the center of the room directly below the opening in the ceiling. I set up the table with the spotlight below it. Next, I placed the red transparency and the six transparent sheets of the drawings on the glass table. I looked at Clare and gave her a thumbs up. Our plan was now ready to be put into motion. We both knew that we were in uncharted territory. Whatever was about to happen, it would put to bed our questions about the markings and we could move on and chalk this up as a great adventure.

My anxiety was building as I reached for the spotlight switch and turned it on. It sent a red beam of light upwards to the oculus. We were crouched in front of the small table, waiting, but not knowing exactly what we were waiting for.

Minutes passed and I leaned over to Clare and whispered, "We can give it another ten minutes and if nothing happens, we'll call it quits, and not give this any more of our time. We can just relax wait till morning and enjoy the rest of our stay in Rome."

She nodded in agreement. I was almost relieved that nothing happened because we had not really thought through what we would do if something did happen. At this point, I was thinking that the experiment was a failure and that we would never find out what these symbols and markings meant. After ten more minutes, I turned off the light, folded up the table and gathered all the equipment that we had brought. As we walked towards the alter to stuff it in Clare's purse something unexpected happened. We could hear a low-level humming sound. We looked up and through the opening we could see a dark shape with a dim string of lights. We looked at each other in absolute terror. Clare gasped and then covered her mouth with her hands as if trying to muffle whatever sounds she may be making. She looked like she had just seen a ghost. Trying not to appear frightened, I shrugged my shoulders as if this sort of thing happens every day. In reality, I was terrified. I found myself wondering what type of demonic force we had unleashed and had we taken this too far.

Clare stood up and looked straight up at the opening. Suddenly a strange tingling sensation went through my body. I felt like I was melting. When I looked at Clare, I was stunned. She seemed to be dissolving. At this point I realized that the strange sensation was actually my body melting away. That was the last memory I had of the Pantheon. The next thing that I remembered was being in a different location with Clare. I looked around and we were surrounded by smooth, glowing, metal surfaces rather than the architectural details of ancient Rome. There were no windows, doors, lights or features of any sort. We were in a barren, metal world.

I looked at Clare, and whispered, "Are you alright?"

She nodded her head and said, "I am but where the hell are we?"

Trying to relieve the tension, I made a feeble attempt at humor and replied, "I don't know but I don't think we're in Kansas anymore. Do you think we can get back to Rome if we click our heels?"

When I did not get the customary laugh that I expected from Clare, I decided that the only good news at this point was that we were both still alive.

Suddenly, I heard a voice say, "Greetings Earthlings. Welcome to your transporter. Do not be afraid. We will not harm you. You are being transferred to the mothership. This will only take a moment."

My first thought was that we were on a Hollywood movie set. Perhaps we had been captured by the authorities and this was some sort of mind game that they were playing with us as a form of punishment. We had violated their sacred space and they were going to be cruel with their response.

Struggling to get the words out of my mouth, I uttered, "Hello."

The male voice said that we must have questions about where we are, and who they were. The person said that we would be provided with answers once we meet in person. Clare and I just looked at one another, unable to speak. It did not feel like we were moving, so maybe this was just a prank. Within minutes, I watched as Clare once again dissolved and the two of us reappeared in another place. We were in a larger space where the walls were draped with flashing lights that continually changed color. Again, it was a stark metal room, devoid of furniture, fixtures, and any defining features. Only a large screen with an image of outer space filled with stars and constellations broke the monotony of the steel walls. We eventually realized that the screen was a window and that we were actually moving through space past the stars and constellations.

The voice announced that we were now on the mothership and we were being transported to their galaxy and their planet. So many questions were running through my head, but I was too stunned to articulate them. If these people were aliens, would we ever see our home again? Had we disturbed the intergalactic order with our experiment? Was Clare's colleague actually an alien and did he deliberately lead us here? There were so many questions racing through my head and so few answers. Clare just stood still, staring at me, not uttering a word.

And then, as minds will sometimes do in moments of extreme stress, I looked at Clare and quietly said, "Arrivederci Roma."

She replied, "Hello to a galaxy far, far away."

We continued the trip terrified and in total silence.

Chapter XIII
WELCOME EARTHLINGS

We continued our intergalactic voyage in stunned silence. We gazed out of what we assumed was a large window that had now expanded to completely encircle us. We could see in every direction, left and right, up, and down. It looked like we were shooting through space, and yet it felt like we were standing still. I looked for Earth but we had moved into another realm. The comfort we would have been able to take from at least having a visual of what we knew as home was long gone. Above us were what I thought to be quasars, below were spinning galaxies and ahead we could see streaks of light as we passed through meteor showers. Had we been at an immersive presentation of outer space it would have been spectacular. However, due to our frightening circumstances, we were unable to appreciate the beauty. We were merely able to process it.

We eventually approached a large sphere that seemed to grow in size as we moved closer to it. Blues, whites, and reds radiated from the surface. Three smaller spheres were orbiting around it. Way off to our left, was a sun radiating light. Amazingly, there seemed to be another sun like sphere way off to the right. There appeared to be galaxies spinning around these suns on a ninety-degree plane to the planet we were approaching.

Finally, I was able to speak and uttered, "Clare, this is amazing."

She did not reply. She just stood and stared out the window.

As we approached the large sphere, I could see oceans, land, and an atmosphere. Off in the distance I could see what I assumed were satellites, and massive fixtures that looked like manufacturing facilities floating in space. They penetrated the atmosphere like huge square straws, with a bulbus structure in the middle surrounded by wings or panels. Occasionally a speeding space craft flashed by. Suddenly, our window to the universe disappeared and we watched as a section of the wall evaporated. We stepped forward into a massive space filled with aviation style crafts. While the majority of the spacecraft were saucer like, others were triangle shaped. They were assorted sizes and none of them had wings.

It was at this point that we saw the first signs of life. The inhabitants were moving about doing what appeared to be maintenance work. These beings resembled humans but had more pronounced features. Their eyes were larger but not grotesque. Their ears seemed small and shaped like a receptor. Their bodies were similar to our bodies, but less muscular. Their hands and feet were similar but smaller. Their skin color ranged from a light to a medium tone and seamed adjust as they moved about. They were dressed in uniforms made of materials similar to hemp or bamboo. The various facial appearances and body types made me think that there was more than one gender.

By this time I was not sure if I was still breathing. My initial terror had put me into an almost catatonic state, just staring and trying to absorb what surrounded me. Two of the alien looking beings approached us and asked if we enjoyed our trip. I could hear their words but I could not see their lips moving.

Dumbfounded, I answered, "It was ok."

They smiled and reached for the equipment and transparencies that I still held in my hands. I pulled off my gloves and balaclava. Without uttering a word, Clare followed my lead, just staring at me in utter shock. Next a delegation of six beings in formal attire approached us. They looked more official than the first two beings we had encountered.

A voice in my head said, "Welcome to Zxentrux."

It occurred to me that one of them had sent the message telepathically, because no one had actually spoken. I wondered if Clare received the same message. They smiled warmly and did not appear to be hostile.

I replied, "Thank you, but what are we doing here?"

They told us to follow them and we would be debriefed. They sensed our terror and said that we have nothing to fear. Again, it was not through spoken words, but it was transmitted through a voice in my head. They led us through the facility and soon we were moving through a tunnel. The walls were decorated with artwork, portraits, and strange writing. The only light was a glow radiating from the surfaces. We entered a room with panoramic views of the outside world. It was stunning. Green vegetation was growing up the walls of the buildings and hanging off the roofs. There were thickets of broadleaf trees and green ground cover instead of grass. It was beautifully manicured and it looked like an artist's rendition of what a perfect landscape would look like. Narrow canals of water wound their way through the structures and vegetation. People and robots were traveling along winding passageways. Some inhabitants were walking, others were riding on floating devices, while others were in enclosed bubble-like vehicles moving along about six inches above the roadways. I noticed that the roads or passageways were made of materials that were not pavement or concrete. The robots were floating on a cushion of air. Occasionally larger freight type vehicles hovered past us. I could not see any light standards or telephone poles. My guess was that we were in some sort of industrial park that was occupied by commercial operations.

We were eventually led to a room with a large table surrounded by ergonomically structured chairs and we were asked to take a seat. The lead delegate began to send us telepathic signals. I was fascinated by how the words could be implanted in my head rather than hearing them with my ears. We sat without speaking and yet we were communicating. At this point I asked if they were able to speak with their mouth and listen with their ears. The spokesperson assured us that they could speak and listen like we do because they have studied and learned the languages of our planet. It was at this point that they began speaking to us using their mouth.

The person started by saying, "Please forgive us. It has been centuries since we have used our lips to speak. Our civilization developed technology that allows us to send brain waves to one another. By doing so, physical, and neurological speech disorders are not an impediment. Everyone can communicate with one another on an even plane. It reduces the amount of energy we have to expend to live our daily lives. Our children still use speech until they reach maturity."

Amazed, I replied, "That is so different from Earth. If we told someone that we were hearing voices in our head, they would deem us insane and institutionalize us."

Once again, I asked where we were and why they brought us here. I assumed the person who was speaking was a woman because she had female features and a feminine voice. Her hair style and attire seemed more lady-like than the others. She told us her name was Isla and asked what our names were. It was like she was trying to get to know us, and she was using the same introductory process that we used on Earth.

She said, "You are on Zxentrux which is light years away from your planet. We brought you here because you summoned us with a request for help."

"How did I do that?" I asked. "Are you saying the light that I shined on you was a call for help? Is it that simple to summon someone on an alien planet?"

She abruptly changed the subject by asking if we would like something to eat or drink. Clare spoke up and said that she would really appreciate water or a snack. The woman pressed a circle on the table.

She then looked at us sympathetically and said, "You have had a long day and you must be very tired. Would you like to freshen up before we continue? I promise that I will answer all your questions and return you to your planet afterwards, unharmed. First, enjoy these snacks."

Almost immediately a clay platter holding goblets of water and strange looking pieces of food was placed in front of us by a short rolling robot. We each reached for a container of water. After taking a sip, we looked at one another in amazement and remarked that it tasted more refreshing and had so much more flavor than water usually does. I asked the woman what made it so uniquely good. She told us that it was just fresh spring water. Nothing was added to enhance the taste.

Clare looked at the unidentifiable bits of food and asked what they were.

The woman replied, "These are crippets. They are made of organic plant matter and fruit. You will like it once you try it."

Clare took a bite and her eyes lit up with amazement.

She said, "These are ridiculously good. This might sound crazy, but I felt a little burst of energy the moment I swallowed it."

The woman explained that they had developed natural health boosting plants. At this point, I bit into one of the snacks, and told Clare that I felt the same jolt of energy.

The woman said that tonight we would be their guests and we could continue our conversation tomorrow. She said there would be much to see and talk about the following day. At this point, one of the delegates that was seated at the table stood up and motioned us to follow him. We thanked her for her hospitality and followed the guide out of the room. We walked through a tunnel that led us outdoors to where a vehicle was waiting for us. The warmth of the summer air smelled so fresh that it almost tasted sweet. The vehicle was a light blue color with a bubble-like top made of glass. There were no wheels and no apparent doors visible. The side of the vehicle opened up and inside were two seats that faced each other. I thought to myself that this must be their version of a limousine except there was no driver.

The guide programmed our destination and the vehicle took off. We hovered out of the industrial park and entered a more urban environment as we moved past other similar vehicles. We encountered a much larger vehicle filled with passengers. It made a stop where beings were waiting to board. I realized that it must be a bus. The streets were exceptionally clean with vegetation and water features with people moving about tending to their affairs. The signage on the buildings seemed more artistic than informative. The murals were portraits, three-dimensional artwork and in some cases the images were animated. There were intersections that were roundabouts and others that went underneath the cross streets. I noticed that overtaking another vehicle was done by levitating up and over the vehicle, then back down again. We passed districts that resembled our own architecture but it looked as though they were being converted to a more nature inclusive environment. I noticed a large beaming sun over to one side and a much smaller one on the distant horizon. I got a sense of peacefulness as we travelled through the streets. Even the people moving about looked relaxed. If they were in a hurry or anxious, it did not look like it.

The vehicle suddenly made a turn and then stopped at a structure that I surmised must be our hotel. It was built into a cliff with large glass windows facing a pool of water. We pulled up under a canopy and then exited the vehicle. We followed a guide into the building. The lobby was grand with natural rock formations and vegetation. A waterfall dropped from a rock ledge into a pool that emptied into a larger pool outside the building through an opening in the wall. The ceiling had stalactites hanging from it. He checked us in and told us we could now proceed to our room. As he was about to depart, I asked him for the keycard. A voice sounded in my head telling me that we have been identified and that the room would open upon our arrival. I wondered how the lock identified us. Was it by our appearance, scent, body temperature or was it something so unheard of that I could not fathom how it was done?

We made our way to the glass enclosed elevator. There was no visible mechanical means of moving the elevator. As soon as we entered, the door closed and launched us upward to our floor. It was like the elevator had a mind and knew where to take us. Searching for our room, we passed robots that we assumed were the cleaning staff. When we arrived at our room, the door automatically opened when we stood in front of it. Entering we found a spacious suite with a breath-taking view below us. We moved to the window and gazed intently at the beauty below. There were mountains in the far-off distance covered in trees. We could see structures peeking out from under the greenery and an ocean of turquoise with sparkling white beaches. Recreational watercrafts were slipping through the waves. Sailing vessels were off in the distance. Birds were floating through the beautiful blue and white hued skies. The scene was breathtaking and filled us with a sense of serenity even though we were in a foreign galaxy on a planet we had never heard of. Our surroundings brought us a sense of calm. We felt safe even when our instincts told us we should be terrified of the unknown.

We finally sat down and looked incredulously at one another. Clare was the first to speak.

She looked at me, smiled, and quietly said, "Jim, if this is real and not a crazy dream, this is the best vacation we have ever been on. It is simply out of this world."

Cautiously, I replied, "I don't know what we have gotten ourselves into, but so far, so good. No one will ever believe this story. It was scary at first but they seem like incredibly good people, and I use the term people very loosely."

After the initial shock of being transported to another planet, it was comforting that we could still look at the humor in the situation, no matter how dire it may be. I knew in that instant, that we would be okay.

We assessed our very peculiar predicament and decided the people and this planet appeared to be an upgraded version of ourselves. They seemed incredibly intelligent and knowledgeable. They were familiar with Earth and did not seem to see us as an enemy. We decided that the hospitality we had been shown was genuine and that we would not be walking into a trap the next morning.

We both needed a shower and clean clothes. It had been a long time since we dressed ourselves that last morning in Rome. Clare opened the closet door to see if there was anything inside that we could change into. Sure enough, there was clothing that was of excellent quality and made for comfort. In the shower, we found a full body spray chamber with a touch screen to change the water temperature and intensity. The settings also provided a choice of four types of soap and shampoo. We quickly realized that the water already had soap in it, so all we needed to do was scrub our bodies with a natural coral sponge and wash our hair with the same soapy water. When I turned the shower off, a gentle blast of warm air enveloped my body and dried me off. Once the cycle was complete, the shower door opened. I felt like I had just run myself through a car wash.

After our shower we tried on our new threads.

Clare looked at me, and in her best Marlena Dietrich voice said, "You look marvelous dawling."

I replied, "You look smashing yourself. Now let's find ourselves something to eat. I am really hungry."

We opened the mini fridge and found a variety of options. There were bottles of liquids and unrecognizable mini snacks. Nothing looked familiar and the descriptions were not printed in English so we had to decide based solely on the appearance of the food. We decided to live dangerously and try the drink in the purple bottle. Opening it was a challenge. The design was so simple it made it difficult to open. It did not have a cap, the top of the bottle just flipped open.

Clare took the first sip and remarked, "This is really good. It tastes like it has alcohol in it but I can't be sure. Here, try it."

She handed the bottle to me and I filled two glasses. We pulled our chairs to the window and admired the view while we sipped on our un-identified liquid beverage and munched on our unrecognizable snacks.

Daylight was turning to dusk and we decided to venture out and find someplace to eat. Back in the lobby, I approached the front counter and asked for a recommendation. The desk clerk sent me a tele-pathic message to let me know that he did not understand what I was saying. When I asked him if he could use his voice to communicate, he raised his index finger and disappeared through the wall behind him.

Suddenly another person appeared and that person sent me a message that I did understand. He apologized for the first clerk, explaining that he did not speak our language. When I asked him if he would mind speaking, he obliged. He explained that we were a unique couple on their planet and not everyone would be able to communicate in our native language.

He looked at us intently and said in a monotone voice, "My name is Slec, and I have studied other worlds in my learning portfolio. What you refer to as college or university is known as portfolio on my planet. In my studies, I found your planet intriguing. I am happy to serve you and apologize for those on this planet that are not familiar with your ways and speech."

I replied, "Thank you Slec. My name is Jim and this is my wife Clare."

"It is a pleasure to meet both of you," he said. "I am aware that on your planet you conduct a ceremony, a contractual bond called marriage between two people that is in effect for the balance of one's life. It is a bit different here."

He explained that on this planet they have developed a form of conjugal union that legally commits two people for a period of five to ten solar transitions. The parties must enroll in an exploration course where all aspects of a union are thoroughly reviewed. This includes lessons about living in a union, having offspring, legal obligations, and resolutions at their disposal. He said they believe that such a serious union must be entered with both parties being knowledgeable. This gives them all the information they need to make good decisions. At the conclusion of each of these periods, a thorough analysis is performed between the two parties through an authorized and certified mediator to determine whether the union is weak and should be dissolved, or strong enough to continue the commitment for another period of five to ten solar transitions. The family of the party participates in the process and the final decision.

Clare blurted out, "What if there are children?"

Slec said that offspring play a significant role in the analysis. If the parents are not willing or capable of continuing in the union there are a series of steps that must be taken to ensure that both parents remain involved in the decision-making process regarding the children through established protocol. There are sometimes contentious issues that need to be resolved but it allows all interested parties to have a stake in the final settlement.

"What happens to the assets of the union?" I asked.

He said that every asset of an unsuccessful union would be resolved at this point. Just like on Earth, there were no perfect solutions when love and commitment had to be negotiated. They have accepted legal means of resolving issues that the parties are not willing to compromise on. There are penalties for breaking union commitments prior to the assigned period which are clearly defined. They have found that this form of union has reduced abuse and abandonment on their planet. Successful unions mean that public funds can be allocated more effectively. He said their system also assists citizens in what we refer to as the golden or retirement years. This gives the elderly an opportunity to rearrange their lives if they so desire after raising their offspring and as they advance in transition years. He told us that the average life span on Zxentrux is approximately 125 transitions or years.

He said affairs of the heart are not always easily resolved through mathematics and science and sometimes require more social means. He said they are guided by their Tezu. The system sounded interesting and effective on Zxentrux, but I did not see how it could solve the domestic problems that we have on Earth. Our solutions are guided by strong religious and legal principles that must be adhered to.

I asked Slec if his people believe in God. His reply was not surprising. He said they believe in a God that created all living things through the unleashing of a force well beyond their capabilities of understanding. This was followed by the formation of the conditions which brought life to various parts of his universe.

Slec continued to speak with clarity and deliberation, "Our God is called Tezu which translates to the word light in your language. We feel that it is our duty to preserve the gifts received by almighty Tezu and to give thanks and love to one another. I have studied your different religions and find confusion among the different dictates has created strife on your planet."

Nodding my head, I said, "You have read the situation on our planet correctly. We have been fighting wars for centuries in the name of whatever God or deity that we believe in. We do not have one clearly defined God and it has brought mayhem, despair, and destruction to our planet rather than peace and serenity. It makes no sense."

Slec said that at the beginning of time they had different versions of Tezu, but with enlightenment and the evolution of technology, they have ascertained that there is only one Tezu. The people of their planet have accepted the findings, and this acceptance and worship of one uniform God has helped to end discord and this in turn, allows them to concentrate all their resources and efforts to care for and advance their society. He said that this harmony has taken generations to achieve by consolidating the different versions of the Tezu basic teachings.

We thanked him for the enlightenment and the time that he took to help us understand his world. By this point, we were famished and quickly changed the subject and asked him where he would recommend that we go for dinner. He quickly suggested the facilities in the hotel. He said the chef was the best in their world and offered to walk us through the menu. We realized that to venture outside of the hotel could mean a language barrier, frustration to communicate, and disappointment with our dinner choice.

"Slec, how do we pay for things here? What is the currency?" I asked.

He replied, "The two of you have been designated guests of the Council. All of your expenses will be taken care of while you are here."

As we followed him through the lobby to the dining room, we noticed that the lights brightened as we approached and dimmed as we moved away. The area appeared to be on motion sensor lights. We were then led through a kaleidoscope of color that encircled us and seemed to move with us until we reached a space that resembled, sounded, and smelled like a tropical forest. Tables shaped like palm trees seemed to be randomly scattered throughout the area. Slec motioned us to a table beneath a large tree. He said he would explain the menu and the server would instinctively know when to return to take the order. The spectacular view that we had been admiring began to change and we were now seated on a cliff overlooking a white mountain range. The restaurant was breathtaking and he could tell by our reaction that we were impressed.

I looked incredulously at Slec and asked, "How do you put something like this together? I have never seen anything like this at home. I just can't wrap my mind around how you can even get this to work."

He explained that they used lasers and holograms to create the different environments that are meant to induce a sense of relaxation and being at one with nature. Slec touched the tabletop and a menu appeared on the surface. He explained in great detail what each item was and then with a second tap on the menu name, a picture of the item appeared so we could have a visual of what we were about to eat. He recommended their finest brog, which he explained is the equivalent of our wine. I asked him what the liquid in the purple bottle in the hotel room was. He said it was one of their finest, light alcoholic beverages made from the quonco fruit which was plentiful on their planet. Slec then excused himself and told us to enjoy our meals.

Within minutes the server brought us two tall glasses of brog. Clare chose an entrée of mixed vegetables in a light-colored sauce and I ordered a plate of fish and a root type vegetable. Once the server left with our order, Clare and I raised our glasses and clinked them together.

Totally serious, Clare said, "I really don't know what we are toasting because I don't know if this experience is actually real. I feel like we are in a fantasy land. It is beyond beautiful here and everyone is gracious. It's like we are living a science fiction version of the Wizard of Oz and we have found the Emerald City."

I replied, "What puzzles me is that we are obviously different from everyone else here, and yet we are not viewed with suspicion and we are able to move around freely without security watching our every move."

Clare suggested that someone could be watching us through a crystal ball. I agreed that somehow, they had to be keeping an eye on us, but however they were doing it, we were oblivious to it. We guessed that they probably had devices tracking our every move but they did not seem threatened by our presence. We realized that we were in a world far more sophisticated than Earth and foreign to anything that the two of us had ever experienced. There was nothing that we could do to change the situation, so we decided that we had to trust that they had our best interests at heart and we had to somehow relax and enjoy the experience.

The scenery continued to change from one spectacular landscape to another, intermingled with what looked like tourist attractions and ancient ruins. Our meals arrived and were arranged on the plates with artistic flair. With our first bites, we experienced what I can only describe as culinary ecstasy. The flavors were potent and tantalizing, unlike anything we had ever eaten on Earth. Each bite was a taste sensation and we savored every morsel.

After we finished our dinner, we headed back to the lobby where we once again encountered Slec. When we asked if we could go outside and explore, he told us that we were free to do so and that we would be safe moving about the area. He reached under the counter and handed me an object that looked like a small fob. We were instructed to carry this with us just in case we got lost or needed help. With a press of the button, someone would come to us and assist us with whatever we needed.

We headed to the glass enclosure at the front of the building. The façade faded away as we approached it, and suddenly we were outside. The night air was crisp with a fresh cool breeze. We looked to the skies and saw two moons surrounded by sparkling stars. On one horizon was the tip of a galaxy; on the opposite horizon was a milky way like feature. It was a stunningly beautiful night and I reached for Clare's hand just to be sure she was still by my side. If we were any place on

Earth, this would have been a romantic stroll. In this world that was so unfamiliar to us, it was more like a trip through a museum. We noticed that even the streets were lit with motion sensor devices. A person zipped past us on a levitating device that was emitting a glow lighting her way on the pathway. As she passed us, she smiled and waved, and I sensed an indistinguishable language in my head. I suspected she was saying hello in her language. Glowing vehicles and robots moved by us and once again the road brightened as they approached and then dimmed once they moved past us.

We walked towards the city through gardens, water features, statues, and artwork. The buildings glowed underneath the vegetation that hung from them. There were no light standards, just shimmering illuminated surfaces. It was eerily quiet on the streets, and yet I could feel a vibrancy from all the activity as people moved about the city. Only the occasional hum of a moving devise passing nearby broke the silence. Off in the distance there appeared to be a carnival with colorful rides. As we moved closer, we could hear the sound of music and the excitement of children's voices. It was refreshing to hear in the still night air. Looking up to the heavens, we could see the occasional aircraft flash through the sky without making a sound. They looked more like shooting stars than powerful moving machines.

After a short walk we made our way back to the hotel. Entering the lobby, I looked for Slec. He was by now our self-appointed, unofficial, go to person. We asked him where we could go to get a drink and he pointed us to a dimly lit lounge that served brog and told us what word we needed to use to order the drink. Patrons looked our way as we entered the lounge and sat ourselves down at a table. It was obvious that we were attracting attention and it made us a bit nervous. A server came to our table and took our drink order. When he left, a patron approached us, and using words, greeted us in his language. When I responded in English, he immediately switched to English.

"Welcome to our little corner of the universe. You must be from the planet Earth," he said as he reached out and shook both of our hands. "My name is Gray and I am a course provider. On Earth I would be referred to as a university professor. I teach astronomy but I have also studied your world's history and can speak your languages."

When I asked what languages he could speak, he told me that in addition to English, he was fluent in French, German, Russian, Chinese, and Japanese. He went on to say that he has an advanced mind capable of holding massive amounts of data that can be recalled in a nano second when needed. This technology is offered only to those who want to achieve a higher level of knowledge and are willing to commit the time and resources to study and retain the information. I assumed that what he referred to as technology is what us Earthlings refer to as education. He said that not everyone needed to get this well-educated and it was done by choice, not by external pressure.

Clare and I introduced ourselves and told him where we were from and explained how we managed to arrive here. He listened politely and then waved over a female sitting at another table. He introduced her as his united partner Lacie. After greeting one another, he told us that they have been together for over fifty solar transitions.

I looked at him and said, "That is amazing. You must have renewed your union more than once. Marriages don't usually last that long on Earth. We have been married for twenty-five years and that is rare where we come from."

They sat down and joined us. I asked him what he taught in his astronomy class. He said they studied the universe much like we did in our astronomy courses but the major difference was that their civilization had mapped out a much larger area of the universe than us Earthlings had. Their people existed for thousands of transitions before Earth, so he said they had a head start.

Gray explained, "We have sent exploration missions to the far reaches of the universe and have determined where life exists. We are zeroing in on the edge of the universe or at least we think we are. It is continuously expanding so it is like trying to hit a moving target. We are also homing in on dark matter and how we can harness it."

Fascinated, I told him that our scientists need to tag along with them because they seem much more advanced than we are. He said that we are all a part of a massive space. Although they have not solved the question of how or why it all began, they are far closer than the most knowledgeable scientists on Earth. They believe like we do that it started with a big bang and gaseous clouds, but they are trying to verify it rather than just hypothesize.

When I asked if they have found life on other planets, he said, "Of course, there are other planets with life. Each one is at a different stage of development. We do not want to disturb life on those planets with exploration, so we have taken on the role of mere observers. It is a part of our council's directives that we are not to interfere with life on other planets. We have learned from our past mistakes and bad experiences. In fact we had a horrific experience on Earth. Your people refer to us as UFOs, but on Zxentrux we refer to it as a bungled mission."

Gray explained that their exploration vehicles are not operated by their people, but rather, they are unmanned and operated by robots. He was aware that the United States military has turned UFO sightings into classified information. He said the unidentified sightings on Earth have been their spaceships collecting data. He said they mean no harm, but the sighting of something unexplainable always causes a stir on Earth.

"Such as yourselves, we are always exploring space and launch missions at certain intervals," he explained. "One day when your technology achieves our level of sophistication, you too will be sending out more missions, further and further into the galaxies. So far, we have not found another planet as advanced as ours, but we have found planets that rival your Earth."

I jumped in at this point and asked, "So you do not have plans to interject yourselves into our affairs? For example, would you prevent a nuclear holocaust?"

He looked at me intently and said, "No, we feel that if we involve ourselves in other planets that it will tip the scales of progress and give you weapons that you may not be ready to deal with, especially in the wrong hands. Each planet must adopt their own order and it can take thousands of transitions to achieve maturity. However, it has come to our attention that your planet is heading towards human extinction. We have debated at length whether it is our moral duty to help reverse the trend. We too have experienced the challenges you are now facing but we rose as a united front and overcame them."

He said it was not his place to give us advice on how to save our planet. That would be up to the council. He was certain they would instruct us as to what needed to be done. It was fascinating and at the same time frightening to know that other beings in the universe were aware of the problems we were having on Earth. I wondered which aspect of our lives seemed dire enough for them to beam us up. Although I was curious, I did not press the issue.

We continued discussing the differences and similarities of our planets. We talked about the different countries, religions and ethnicities that existed on Zxentrux and on Earth. I did not have to give him a plethora of information. He knew all about us. He did, however, enlighten us as to life on Zxentrux. Their planet had originally been a world of diverse nations, populations, and languages, thousands of transitions ago. Over the course of time, they managed to achieve a global culture but not always through cooperative means. Throughout their history, they had their struggles, suffered through destructive behavior, and sometimes expressed their differences in barbaric ways. There was prejudice and religious conflict. Thousands of transitions ago, the planet was more of a melting pot, attempting to blend all the differences, varied beliefs, and ethnicities in an attempt to eliminate religious and racial unrest. It took extraordinary means and hundreds of transitions to work together to seek out common ground that would benefit all the inhabitants.

Through time and education, they became more unified. They were now a global community with 162 divisions, each with an elected local council and their own administration. The members of the council are not allowed to hold significant interests in business. In an effort to be totally transparent, and to avoid a conflict of interest, all members are limited to eight percent of their portfolio in non-governmental business. The balance of their portfolio can be invested in council guaranteed certificates that give them a set percent premium over and above the going rate. It is not a perfect system but it works. This gives their inhabitants the incentive to become a member of a council and work together for the global good. Each of the 162 councils is represented in the global council. This was achieved only after they almost destroyed themselves by exploiting the planet's resources and practicing self-destructive behavior. Had they not worked together they would not have achieved the world they now live in. He said the planet would have died.

Gray was a fascinating being to listen to. He said the history of this self-destructive turmoil is taught to every young person in every history class. They want their youth to understand the hardships and resolution that it took to live in this glorious place. The goal was that they would not slack off and once again let the planet die. If that were to happen, all the work that had been done would have been for nothing. They did not want the generations coming up the pike to take what they have for granted. They want them to know that it will take continued challenging work to sustain this way of life. He said that they have preserved past cultures and time periods for educational purposes and to show how much they have evolved from exceedingly challenging times.

His words were both mesmerizing and inspiring. I thought of how hard it is to convince people on Earth that climate change actually exists, let alone take action to stave it off and save the planet. On Earth, saving our planet had become a political issue rather than a common goal. Clare and I took immense pride in our recycling efforts, but after listening to Gray's story, it made me realize that our efforts would not have an impact on reversing global warming. His words made me want to not only do more but put myself in a position to actually inspire others. He made me realize that we have to act, but it would take unified global action to be successful. He said difficult lifestyle changes would have to be made to preserve the beauty of our world.

He was aware of the civil unrest on Earth and said that it still exists on their planet because there are aspects of their society that are not fully represented. Their councils, which consist of four different parties and one elite, deal with these problems. Each party represents an aspect of governance. For instance, they have a party that deals with social issues, one that is liberal, another that is conservative and finally one that is ultra conservative. Each party has equal representation. The one elite position is filled by an outstanding being who has been successful in life. This person is usually one of their wealthier citizens.

They also have a judicial council made up of two judges from each party who deals with issues beyond the council's ability. They have laws similar to those on Earth and they have authorities that enforce them just as we do. There is also a Global security force which is trained but underutilized. He said there is currently great debate as to whether it is even needed. It was part of enforcement as they inched their way towards a global society and council. Its purpose has dwindled and its action is rarely required these days. He said it has been retained because sometimes change is difficult and old ways never die.

Eventually our conversation drifted from historical fact to a more personal level. We learned that Gray's wife Lacie was a member of the Liberal party. In that capacity, she dealt with redevelopment, social programs, and community outreach on the planet. She said her job could get incredibly challenging but with a balanced approach good decisions that were in the best interest of the majority of the population on the planet were usually achievable. She seemed fascinated with our vocations. A president of a company and a bank compliance officer were foreign concepts to her and she pressed us for details throughout the remaining hours of the evening. We shared drinks discussing our families until we realized it was early morning. We stood, shook hands, and thanked one another for the delightful and educational evening.

Once we were safely back in our room, our conversation centered on our friendly companions.

Clare asked, "Do you think they were planted there by the council to keep tabs on us?"

Trying to be pragmatic and not stoke any fear, I answered cautiously, "You could look at it in more than one way. It was either a well thought out strategy to check up on us or it was a purely coincidental meeting with two open-minded and social people. Based on our appearance alone, we stand out in the crowd. They were just as curious about us as we were about them."

Clare noticed a blue flashing light on the wall above the desk and symbols embedded in the wall below it. I walked over, touched the light and a message appeared in English. It read that breakfast was served from 7:00 a.m. to 9:00 a.m. and that our transport would pick us up at 10:00 a.m. Other than the method of delivery, it felt wonderfully familiar. In that moment, we felt like we were staying at a hotel on Earth, and it eased the apprehension that I felt but did not want Clare to see. This was all so bizarre and out of our world strange. We should have been terrified but instead we were just a bit nervous not knowing what lay ahead. We were just taking it all in, moment by moment.

We crawled into bed, and when I laid down the mattress reshaped itself to the contours of my body. It seemed to move as I moved and I noticed that the temperature of the bed would increase if I slipped the covers off of me. Instead of resting, I found myself moving from one position to another to see what the bed would do. I was fascinated. Finally, Clare told me to go to sleep.

Like a stern mother speaking to her child, she said, "Yes, the bed is fascinating. Our entire day was fascinating, but we don't know what is ahead of us tomorrow. We need to sleep and be rested so we will be prepared for whatever we encounter. With all your moving around and reacting each time the bed moves or the temperature changes, I can't get to sleep."

After admonishing me, she put her arms around me, kissed my neck and whispered, "Good night, my bat shit, crazy ass, love."

My dreams relived the events of the day, but in a more fantastical way. It was like I was in a Star Wars movie. I was in a space craft and Jedi fighters were shooting at the enemy. It was the wild west in outer space. We managed to take out our adversary and safely return to the mothership. After travelling through space we landed on Zxentrux.

We were the conquering heroes and there was a massive parade honoring us for defeating the invaders. After thanking us, the lead councilor told the crowd that our next mission would be to destroy the planet Earth. It would be a counterattack for invading the airspace of Zxentrux. I was pleading with the crowd not to destroy Earth, telling them that they are good, kind people that meant no harm and that my family would be destroyed along with the planet. It was at this point that I was arrested, put in shackles, and declared a traitor.

My deep, fitful sleep had been invaded by nightmares. My sense of calm was replaced with panic. Maybe these people are not as nice as they appear. Maybe it is just a ruse to make us feel safe so we do not fight whatever agenda they have planned for us. My thrashing had awakened Clare. After recounting the nightmare, all she had to say was that this one was a doozy. She then told me to go back to sleep and stay out of trouble. She did not seem concerned and was back in her peaceful slumber within minutes. I stayed awake until morning going over and over any details that I could remember about the dream. There was little sleep for me that night, just uneasy thoughts about what would lay ahead of us tomorrow.

Towards daybreak, I gently nudged Clare out of her sleep and asked, "Do you think they will take us home? Do you think we will ever see the kids again and go back to our normal lives?"

Still half asleep she mumbled, "I hope so."

Chapter XIV
ZXENTRUX

I awoke the next morning to the sound of Clare in the shower. The nightmares had ended and it was just the two of us in our new, surreal world. Getting out of bed, I walked to the window hoping the view would be Rome and the previous day was just one exceedingly long, very strange dream. What I saw was not concrete, glass structures and ancient buildings. Rather, what I saw was surreal beauty and greenery. It was a vision of serenity with mountains and water serving as a backdrop. The structures with their smooth lines were covered with vegetation and blended into the landscape. They looked like vertical slabs of groundcover. There were exposed surfaces on the buildings that I assumed were to absorb light. I counted twelve large rectangular sheets of thin material laying horizontally on the rooftops. They were spaced about six inches apart waving in the wind, curling in and out as the wind subsided or picked up. I thought to myself that this must be a wind powered generator. The roads and walkways looped around the structures and I could see people moving about. It was apparent that we were not in Kansas anymore Toto and this was not a dream.

Once again, I found myself worrying about what the day would bring. Clare came out of the bathroom with a towel wrapped around her wet hair.

She seemed to be rested and in good spirits and joked, "I should have brought my makeup bag on this trip."

We laughed and my morning irritability dissipated. She knew me well and after the restless night I had, she knew I needed to be jolted out of my mood with a bit of humor.

She went on to say, "That was an amazing bed. I slept like a baby. Do you think they will let us keep it as a parting gift?"

Clare sat down on the bed and motioned for me to join her. She reassured me that my dream was just a nightmare and she was confident that everything was going to work out well and they would send us back to earth unharmed. I wanted to believe that she was right. When we were interacting with various people, everyone seemed genuinely nice and normal, but once we were in our room, tortured thoughts consumed me. Were they really our friends or our foes? My dream seemed to indicate the latter. It was so confusing. I decided that a hot shower in the human carwash might rid me of my night terrors.

Once we were showered and dressed, we headed downstairs to the breakfast area. It was situated in the hotel complex, but in a different building and quite a distance from the elevator and the lobby. When we arrived at the restaurant, we were met by a host who seated us and touched the table to reveal the morning fare. We scrolled through the menu and clicked on the items we wanted to order. Within minutes, a robot server brought us our drink selection which we hoped was coffee. We took a sip and it was not coffee, but it did have a pleasing earthy flavor. Our food arrived and it resembled a typical breakfast. There were egglike items with strips of something that looked like bacon but did not taste like it. The fruit bowls were made up of several types of produce that were unfamiliar to us. The meal was different but delicious. We sat and watched people come and go. Every so often someone would smile or wave in our direction. Sometimes a garbled message would enter our minds as the patrons attempted to communicate with us in their dialect. To avoid offending anyone, we would wave and smile hoping they were being friendly and not threatening to kill us.

When we left the restaurant, a transporter appeared. The huge doors opened like it was about to devour us. We stepped inside and sat down. It was amazing that on Zxentrux, we did not have to call for an uber or a cab. It was like the transportation system knew when we would need it. I could not decide if they were tracking our movements or if they were tracking our minds. Whichever it was, this system would be good to have on Earth. There would be no more waiting in the rain in harsh weather. There would be no more time wasted waiting for a ride share. Life would be so much easier and efficient. We rode back to our building in silence watching the movement of life on the streets. People were scuttling about and vehicles were merging and passing one another.

Back at the facility, Isla greeted us and asked if we were enjoying our stay. I thanked her for making us feel so comfortable and for the consideration that we have been given.

"I am so impressed with what I have seen here," I said.

"Thank you for noticing," she replied. It has taken a bit of time, trial, and error but we are getting there and our way of life is getting better and better every day. We still have various issues to address but we are determined to work on them until they are resolved."

She led us down a corridor to a meeting room. Four other people entered the room and took their seats. She introduced them as Jix, the head of Space Exploration, Drin, the head of Planet Affairs, Brev, the head of Science and Technology and Rhit, the head of Social Affairs.

Isla was the first to speak once the introductions were done.

She explained, "We have more departments but I thought that these would be of the most interest to you. I am the head of the Central Council made up of 162 councils on this planet."

After introducing ourselves and exchanging pleasantries, I thanked them for their hospitality. When they asked if I had any questions I asked how they were able to transport us out of the Pantheon.

Isla replied, "We have developed a technology that dematerializes the body then reconstructs it again. However, it is only used by our space agency and it is only used to transport objects a short distance. The physics is complex and requires massive energy to perform so we only use it in extreme situations such as the one you experienced. We are continuing our research to develop it further."

Once all of our questions were answered, Isla began the meeting with a history of their planet.

She started the conversation by saying, "Our planet, like Earth, is millions of transitions old. This planet experienced the same beginnings as most others did during the big bang. Life started as microbes and developed into creatures over the millennia. Zxentrux experienced drastic change over extended periods of time. The temperature changed from molten hot to ice cold. As the solar system stabilized, the planet started to develop into a place where life could be sustained. At first only wild animals inhabited our world. Evolution continued for millions of transitions."

She explained that thousands of transitions ago, their ancestors discovered this planet through space exploration and a desperate search to find a pristine environment to replace their dying planet. Their original planet was virtually destroyed by exploitation, greed, and toxic behavior. Their history was not a pleasant one. She said their ancestors pushed the limits of their original planet to the point of no return. The atmosphere was getting so hot that civilization was struggling and dying. The health of the population was in a drastic decline. The waterways and lands had devolved from healthy environments to valleys of death and pools of poison. The average temperature was approaching 120 degrees.

Their civilization was also experiencing horrible unrest and crime as people fought for depleting resources, food, and shelter. Governments were losing control as mass demonstrations and protests were followed by an escalation of property destruction. Nations were invading one another to take control of resources. Water became a valuable commodity, as did fertile land. Wars ensued. Panic and chaos were increasing at a pace similar to the planet's temperature.

Thankfully, the pioneers of the planet recognized that these trends were potentially catastrophic before the population totally destroyed themselves. They developed a strategy and armed themselves with a sharp vision of how to save their planet. Those pioneers were determined not to let their past behavior predict their future behavior. The chaos that she was describing sounded much like the current conditions on Earth. It was as if she was warning us what could lay ahead for our planet without directly saying so.

She said the first step they took to save the planet was to admit that they had failed to preserve it. Previous governments on the old planet were incapable of averting the disaster. Political discord had prevented any type of action. Each country on the planet had their own agenda and cooperation on the environment was impossible despite all the efforts that were made. The population of the world was growing too rapidly, and wars, land grabbing, and isolationism undermined the progress. Eventually, any talk of action to avert disaster ceased. It took an alliance of the wealthiest people who could see their fortunes slipping away to finally act and address what needed to be done. Those who had been contributing to the problem finally awoke and realized that it was time to do something. It was this alliance that crossed geographical boundaries and finally made a difference.

The one percent of the population that held seventy-five percent of all wealth on the planet had agreed to come together and put their money and influence to work to save their world. This group understood the challenge and committed to jointly work with governments and organizations to bring about change. They developed a game plan that was referred to as the twenty-five-transition plan. It meant they had to convince all the planet governments that they were the people who needed to head up the transformation. Along with government financial support and their own wealth they created a global effort with a massive budget. The best scientists and engineers were brought together to tackle the problem. Initially, the plan was to clean up their planet but they quickly realized that it had gone too far to reverse the trend in the brief time frame available. There had been previous bandage efforts to slow the deterioration but they had not been successful. The conclusion was to develop technology for deep space travel and to find a new planet. It took ten transitions to find and develop this planet that was environmentally similar.

She told us that prior to fully populating Zxentrux, the pioneers had to create a set of rules that not only governed the population but also the technology. Before they could move the population from a dying planet to a healthy one, they needed to set the stage for a totally sustainable environment. It took about twenty-five transitions to complete the move. During those twenty-five transitions the pioneers pursued all options to slow the deterioration of the old planet while simultaneously building on the new one. They were fortunate to have found this planet in time. The undertaking was a huge challenge but with the total cooperation of the dying planet's government and inhabitants it was successful. As the old planet lost its life-giving atmosphere, they gradually built and moved the population along with animals, marine life, and plants to this new location. It was somewhat like Noah's Ark.

For a sustainable transition they had to develop a different mindset as to how life would be conducted on the new planet. Governing and business were completely redesigned. Education became a key ingredient to their success. A central agency consisting of marketing experts were tasked with informing every inhabitant of the old planet of the dire situation and the necessary steps that each and every individual would need to take part in. Even though there were still naysayers, the assistance of a very persuasive agency helped the population come together in a unified effort. The twenty-five-transition plan was distributed and translated.

One of the first steps was to make science, technology, environmental studies, and fellowship, requisite courses of study starting at the age of five. By educating the population in science they would understand that their existence depended on these principles in order to be good stewards of the planet. It was imperative that every inhabitant understood that exploitation of the planet had to be replaced with preservation and prevention. They had to initiate practices that not only provided for the necessities of life but would also preserve their environment. People could no longer take for granted that the world they now inhabited would be preserved for their children and grandchildren if they did not take steps to maintain it.

Their first challenge was to reach every single child on the planet and teach the simple concepts of science, technology and environment through play and experiments. This became part of their universal education system. Wireless communications and satellites helped teachers educate children in all corners of the planet. These teachings would continue through to the higher levels of education. Universities were converted and dedicated to environmental studies including bioengineering, science, energy, materials, and fellowship. Temporary schools were built in the far reaches of the planet. She said they still focus on science today, but they also have traditional universities that teach all forms of study so they can produce well rounded citizens of the planet.

Isla said that at the same time, space engineering was developing equipment that could travel at extremely high speeds and for long journeys. Through the use of Artificial Intelligence, they were able to develop innovative ideas at a breakneck pace. Concept to production time was cut tenfold. Every person that had already completed their studies was required to take supplemental studies where they were taught the simple concepts of science and environmental studies. These were prerequisites for immigration to the new planet and a part of the twenty-five transition preparations. It was evident that education alone played a significant role in reducing environmental degradation and changing the population's habits. By educating the entire planet, they were able to establish a focused effort. This helped to create a buffer of time if the twenty-five-transition plan could not be met on schedule.

She explained that this was a period of major struggle as governments had to analyze all forms of emissions and pollution that existed. Tough choices had to be made. Non-essential industries had to reduce or stop production. Unnecessary long-distance travel had to be cut back severely. The entire planet was put on a life altering diet. Food was distributed evenly and consumption of non-essentials was drastically reduced. Fossil fuels were used only for crucial needs. The use of power and lighting were critically analyzed. Governments agreed to halt all military production, training and exercises, and non-aggression agreements were signed. The armed forces from every nation were employed in the effort to reduce consumption, help feed the planet, establish education, quell unrest, and prepare for the transfer. They were unprecedented times. It was a fight for survival and everyone had to play a part. The inevitable could no longer be delayed. Posturing, denial and pushing the problem further down the road was no longer an option. They had hit rock bottom. It was unfortunate that it took an extreme, dire situation to prompt action when a little prevention could have avoided the entire disaster.

When Isla paused for a moment, I jumped in and said, "The parallels to what Earth is going through right now are uncanny. Unfortunately, we are still in the destruction phase with our heads buried in the sand. We think we are doing our part by recycling, bicycling, turning the heat down and the air up, but after listening to you, I realize that we are not doing enough to save our planet. Despite extreme weather and fires, I don't think our wealthiest citizens or government are ready to make drastic changes. Those who could initiate the transformation and have profound influence seem to be driven by greed and self-preservation."

She said she was aware of that and continued with her lecture. Beyond education, they had to change their constitution to clearly identify this new way of governing and how representation would be achieved. This was why the council system was created. I told her that I was familiar with the system and about our chance meeting with Gray. She seemed to know him and said that Gray is well respected and is someone that they refer to often in regard to space exploration. She said we were fortunate to have met him.

Before this new planet was populated there was a thorough analysis of all technologies that could reduce toxic byproducts. They knew they could not totally eliminate them but felt they could manage them. Biology played a significant role in this planet's development. Scientists determined that nature's balance needed to be respected. Every technological center was critically analyzed to determine its environmental score. A scale of severity was implemented to analyze the processes that were used to create products. Minimum levels of harm to the planet had to be maintained. Any technology that did not meet the required standards needed to submit to a series of recalculations until it could meet the required target. Failure was not an option. Those who could not or would not meet the minimum target were not allowed to proceed with production and were forced to pursue alternatives.

Once technologies passed scrutiny they were certified for operation and gradually the new planet was developed and populated. Isla said their ancestors were on a very tight schedule and needed to develop innovative methods in order to save the planet's inhabitants. Fortunately, they were successful and were able to move the entire population.

Since then, they have used the old planet as a proving ground to evaluate recent technology that could clean up the environment. She said they are determined and dedicated to fixing a past wrong. It would take a considerable amount of time and effort to reverse the damage to the previous planet but they were committed to doing so. She said that much of their heritage is still on that planet and they hoped to repopulate it one day.

After the mayhem and destruction that took place on their original planet, their ancestors decreed that their new planet would be one that worked with nature, not against it. They learned how to reduce waste through science and technology. Builders, developers, and governments had to offset any destruction of natural vegetation with an equal amount of nature regeneration. For every tree that was cut down, an equal number of similar trees had to be planted in Council owned property such as parks, forests, and urban areas. Water features were treated the same way. Each new development had to provide two years of care for the relocated features and provide a four-year maintenance deposit to the council. If the two-year period ended in success the four-year deposit was returned to the developer. This added to the initial cost of the development but it saved the environment.

Isla said that buildings have to meet environmental standards. Each material produced must have a carbon value. Fossil fuels are almost non-existent on Zxentrux. They have developed computer intelligence that can calculate the carbon value of an entire build. Then the builder and developer, in conjunction with the government have to offset that value by means at their disposal. This is a required part of the permitting process that cannot be bypassed. The planet's creed is to add to nature or pay a fee to balance out the carbon footprint. The carbon offset balance is used to improve existing technology and develop innovative equipment that reduces carbon and toxins in the atmosphere. The developer can also reduce the fee by making the structure self-sufficient and totally recyclable. This can be achieved by installing wind or solar energy and water filtration and recycling.

I was fascinated by their ingenuity and was spellbound as Isla continued to speak about how they grappled with what we call climate change and won. She said there was not an area in their world that was untouched. This line of thinking even applied to the transportation industry. Their computers have been used to develop materials which require less waste and polluting by-products. They have developed compression conversion technology for plastics, thus transforming massive quantities of plastics into highly compressed solid materials which can be used in other products. Additive production or 3D processes are used in all aspects of manufacturing and building.

They have also developed methods where soil becomes an integral part of construction. Their structures add ground surface and vegetation which breathes and purifies the air. She said they have developed clinical photosynthesis. Their products are engineered using renewable resources. They still use materials such as wood and plastics but they have learned to offset the damage caused by using them. From clothing to food, all matter must pass rigorous examination prior to release.

They have developed vertical farming and efficient food production through engineering and are growing almost seventy-five percent of their food by organic means using composting. Isla said that research continues on ways and means of reducing waste and improving purification. Their packaging must be biodegradable or convertible so they can compost it or use it as a building material. They have minimized recycling through biodegradable engineering. She continued to say that even their health care has experienced significant improvements due to the changes they have made. With a cleaner environment, health issues have been drastically reduced and health care costs have plummeted.

Isla said one of their greatest achievements has been the development of motion efficiency. They harnessed electromagnetism which is a planet's natural force of energy through quantum mechanics. They no longer need propulsion to move objects. Through the use of laser and radio wave technology, they can now project electromagnetic and electrical fields and move through space at unimaginable speed thanks to lower friction in the vacuum of space. Scientific discovery helped them harness the forces between an atom and a nucleus. She said each transporter has a mini fusion reactor aboard. Fusion leaves no radioactive footprint but produces massive energy to convert to electromagnetism.

Similar to what we have done on Earth, they started out with fission nuclear power which created radioactive issues. After too many accidents they realized that they needed to find a better source of energy. Their transporters can now travel longer distances in shorter periods because of this, and they can change direction rapidly. They do not send citizens in their space crafts on their exploration missions. All their transporters are controlled by computers and robots that are programmed to travel, examine, and avoid confrontation.

Their ground vehicles run on roads made of materials that absorb sunlight, which is then converted to magnetic force which helps to propel the vehicles that are also magnetized. The roads can produce power for lighting and energy storage. Again, fusion reaction provides energy during dark periods. She said that wind and sun power is still preferred to this because it is more economical for the average person. On a grander scale their atmosphere is orbited by solar panels producing power that is directed back to the planet via radio waves. All of this did not evolve overnight, but it did happen rapidly because of the life and death urgency of the planet.

She said the social order is also a part of the environmental effort. They realized in earlier years that excessive consumption and explosive commerce contributed to atmospheric degradation. The over population of the planet contributed to the overall environmental destruction. She said it has been statistically studied and proven that higher education leads to better decision-making about family and life in general. Education has contributed to a decrease in family size. Robots have been integrated into their society to help offset the reduced population growth.

Isla explained that similar to Earth, Zxentrux has laws that protect people's rights, and statutes that regulate communications and media. Beyond that, they also have laws governing the type and functionality of Artificial Intelligence and robots. Science and medical advancements are closely monitored to avoid genetic over engineering and virus development. One of their advancements involves the recording of all the information that resides in the brain. They are able to download memory onto a data bank and use this technique to preserve information from their greatest minds before they retire or pass away. This new order does have challenges and they still struggle with citizen issues but for the most part, lives are much better now than they were back thousands of transitions ago. She said the average lifespan is at least one hundred transitions. Business and independent council continue working together to adopt environmental solutions. Isla said they are confident that they can sustain their planet for generations to come.

She said they have placed limits on the accumulation of wealth. A lifestyle of comfort and privilege is not discouraged, but it has to have limits. She said this may sound like socialism but it was necessary in order to avoid past transgressions. She said that excessive affluence has proven to be destructive. A strong economy occurs when money moves around and is fluid rather than accumulating in financial institutions in the hands of a few individuals. Scientists and economists have determined that uncontrolled wealth is a danger to the environment and the economy. Historically, they found that extremely rich individuals eventually lost touch with the damage they were causing. In contrast, they also realized that wealthy individuals wanted to leave a positive legacy, so they encouraged them to do so within the framework of planet protection. She said they still believe that incentives must remain in place to build wealth and achieve a higher standard of living but it had to be within predetermined constraints. Therefore, all 162 councils were called upon to determine the upper limits of wealth. This would give the businessperson or entrepreneur a frame of reference or a goal. She said they find this system actually helps the individual live a fuller life. Their average citizen's wealth is constrained through their pay structure and their subsequent ability to invest. They felt the super affluent sector of the population should also have these limits.

Wealth can only exceed the prescribed limits if the excess is turned over to carbon offset balance or to the citizen equality budget, which helps to redistribute capital. The equality budget works to prevent poverty by making sure that education is available to all children. Food is distributed from these funds to ensure those who need it get proper nutrition. No one should go hungry. Easy access to food and education has proven to reduce suffering, unrest, and inequality. She said they find that this approach gives everyone an opportunity to seek out employment and possibly start a business because they can live without fear of food insecurity. She said that philanthropic contributors are given special treatment and global recognition. They are often given the council approved opportunity to name government structures. Even these privileges have limits and are monitored and enforced through their taxation and blockchain system.

What she said next shocked me. She referred to Dale Carnegie. She said that he was a good example of someone on Earth that was a major contributor to pollution but changed his ways and eventually became a philanthropist. It was amazing that someone on Zxentrux was so aware of individuals on Earth.

It was at this point that I interjected and said, "You know Isla, the ancient tribes had it right. They were community focused taking care of both young and old. They worked with nature and preserved their culture. When progress arrived, it destroyed that balanced approach by exploiting not only nature but man as well."

Isla agreed and moved on. She said that start-ups are encouraged on Zxentrux and they have venture capitalists who help fund eco-friendly innovations. Companies are limited to a prescribed maximum size to avoid monopolies. Once a business achieves a specific level of asset value it must start another separate company in a different location. This prevents the concentration of business and industry in one area and they believe that it limits massive waste. It also helps to monitor and moderate bad business practices. They try to discourage larger organizations from franchising smaller companies. They feel that this helps to keep the wealth distributed among the population.

She then told us they had discovered that the nitrogen in the Earth's atmosphere acts as mini depositories of knowledge and information. Breathing nitrogen in and out leaves minute deposits of incoherent knowledge left behind by previous individuals who also breathed it in and out. It appears to be random and also dependent on location. She said that nitrogen moves about and can travel from one location to another. It is like random bites of computer programming circulating in the air. As you accumulate more of these random bites, they can formulate a thinking process. Again, this is predicated on randomness and location.

In their explorations, they were able to accumulate a quantity of nitrogen. They filtered and condensed it and then mapped minute pieces of information that seemed to fit together. The one and only time that they affected earth they conducted experiments by harvesting air around Earth until they found logic. She said that after the experiments were completed, they released the nitrogen samples and it is quite possible that Albert Einstein and Nikola Tesla inhaled those samples. She said they believed this to be true because these experiments took place during their eras on Earth. Judging by the advancements in technology on our planet, even though they have no proof, they suspect that those nitrogen strings have been making the rounds. She said they see it as a way of paying knowledge forward. After that experiment we resolved to no longer influence other planets with our discoveries.

The more she spoke, the more I felt like I was on overload. The information she was giving us was mind blowing. I barely had time to process one chain of information before she moved on to another. What was remarkable was that she was not reading from a whiteboard or presenting information on a projector. She was drawing this overabundance of data from her mind without any type of prompt or visual aide. The information she gave us made sense of what we considered unexplainable on Earth. These people were obviously of a superior intellect and far more innovative than we were. I wished that she would give us a paper handout or a memory stick to take back to Earth for future reference.

She said that she would like to show us their innovations. She asked us to follow her to the transporter area where a vehicle awaited us. After entering, we sunk ourselves into ultra-comfortable seats with Isla and her entourage. It was nothing like our trip to Zxentrux where we were forced to stand. We could barely feel that the vehicle was in motion and within minutes we were exiting at a large facility that looked like an expansive plateau of vegetation. Isla explained that this was the central fusion plant which also contained the central data center. We entered the brightly lit facility. The first thing we saw were what appeared to be endless rows of data banks. The facility was sparce and spotless with only a few people moving about. Next, we moved to the fusion reactors. I estimated that there were about one hundred reactors clustered together, all quietly producing energy. Isla said they have thousands of these facilities throughout Zxentrux.

After about forty-five minutes of touring, she led us back to the transporter.

"How do you distribute power to all your users?" I asked.

Once again, as if she was reading it from a book, she expanded on the subject. She said they have developed a method of wireless power transmission. It took a significant amount of engineering and experimentation to accomplish but it has helped to significantly reduce the number of resources needed to energize the planet. Their goal is to always continue to seek better ways to reduce the use of resources. They do not get complacent about innovation just because it is working well. They are always looking to see what they can do to sustain the resource in the future.

She suggested that we move on to another one of their innovations. This time we hovered over a large field of green leafy plants being tended to by robotic equipment going up and down the rows plucking and pruning. There were people who appeared to be monitoring the fields and taking samples. Isla explained that this is one of their outdoor fields that is managed through agrotechnology. Soil management and composting play a significant role in their agriculture. They have improved their yields by fifty percent over the last ten transitions.

Next, we flew over to a massive operation that appeared to be thousands of acres in size. All we could see were rows of glass surrounded by soil. She said that these are internal growing fields that have climate control and are managed by a handful of people and an army of robots. Then she took us to a tall structure covered with vegetation. Panels covered the walls from ground to roof on the side at regular intervals. She told us that they perform vertical agriculture here. The structure was about ten stories high. She explained that inside there are mechanisms operating to provide water and nutrients to stacked fields of fruits and vegetables.

We then sped off to a large area that appeared to be a swamp or a marsh. As we hovered overhead, she explained how they use natural formations to filter water. Wastewater is pumped into the marshy area and then emptied into a large reservoir. There it is held in storage until they send it to their filtration plant and on to water distribution systems.

Isla said we would next be heading out into the atmosphere. We quickly made our way into space and hovered close to a large satellite like object. It was about the size of an automobile with an array of solar absorbing wings. She explained that this is one of their communication satellites that helps to communicate within the planet and with their distant transporters and satellites. We circled it and then moved onto another large floating object that had a very long massive metal tube protruding from the planet's atmosphere and out into space. She said this was a carbon capture satellite. It too had solar capturing wings. She explained that the large bulging section located beyond the atmosphere held the vacuum and power source. Its function was to suck up air from the atmosphere and separate the oxygen from the carbon. The oxygen is returned to the atmosphere and the carbon is dissipated to outer space. This helps reduce carbon in the air. She said this concept was originated on the old planet. Initially every industry that produced carbon was required to install a stand-alone unit at their facility to help neutralize the CO_2 they produced. In the meantime, they built prototypes and had them orbit the old planet and found it successfully accomplished the goal. Unfortunately, the capacity of the old versions could not save the planet in time.

"That's amazing," I responded. "We need something like that on Earth."

Isla agreed and told us that the council was debating whether to send us back to Earth with all the engineering needed to build these units.

Clare had been silently absorbing the deluge of information, but at this point she spoke up and said, "You have our vote."

"The problem is that this would be contrary to our current agreement that states we are not to interfere with other planets," Isla replied.

I told her that I understood, but our planet desperately needed this technology and innovation. She said they were very aware of our predicament, but due to the current political climate on our planet, they were concerned that a hostile response would undermine any assistance that they were willing to give. They were very aware that cooperation is lacking among our world's nations. Another of her concerns was that it could upset their planet's balanced world if Earth's inhabitants sought more innovations from Zxentrux through hostile means. She promised to have an answer before we went home.

Our next stop was a visit to the previous planet of Zxentrux. She explained that we would see what happens to a planet that is void of a sustainable atmosphere. It took about an hour of travel but it passed quickly as we watched the panoramic view zoom by. It became obvious as we neared the planet that there were no signs of life. The surface was red with areas of brown, blue and white. Dark red swirling clouds appeared to hang over large desert expanses. I could see hundreds of the carbon capture units in the atmosphere above the planet. We moved in closer, and evidence of previous habitation started to appear. Old deteriorating structures dotted the surface. Collapsed bridges and buildings were evidence of once thriving cities. Now their only function seemed to be that of obstructing the view of the sand dunes. There were no people, no animals, no forms of life visible. There was no living vegetation to be seen, just dark sticks protruding from the ground in large clusters of what we assumed were once lush green forests. Parts of the surface seemed similar to that of Mars. Isla said the ground temperature was about 150 degrees. It was devastating to see this type of destruction and desolation. It resembled what I imagined the aftermath of nuclear destruction would look like.

We hovered over to a series of structures that appeared to be modern. She said these structures are science labs where studies are currently being conducted. It was here that scientists were monitoring the progress of carbon reduction. It took thousands of transitions for carbon to build up; they hoped it would only take hundreds of transitions to clean it up and bring the planet back to life. When the time was right, vegetation and wildlife would be transported back to this planet, but she said this was a very long-term goal.

Clare and I looked at each other with sadness. Words escaped us. What we had just seen, was what few people on Earth wanted to believe could actually happen to our planet. We were so emotional it caused tears to well up in our eyes. We had just witnessed the aftermath of a slow, agonizing death and resulting devastation due to what we call climate change.

"This is just awful," Clare said wiping away the tears rolling down her face.

I wiped away my own tears and put my arm around Clare. We turned to Isla and expressed our deepest regrets. It was like we were at a funeral. The most frightening thing was that we knew this was a premonition of the demise of our own planet. We both knew in that moment, that all the recycling, composting, organic foods, and reusable bags that we had smugly thought was offsetting climate change was just not enough to save our world. We had to do more. Everyone had to do more.

Isla approached us and gave us a comforting hug.

She said, "Somehow you two need to prevent this from happening on your planet. Somehow you have to find a way to get people to listen. You have seen the carnage and now you have seen the solution. It is up to you."

"I wish I could bring everyone from our planet here to see this. It is so impactful. Sometimes you have to see carnage firsthand to really understand the devastation," I said. "Of course, this could also create a hopelessness that leads us to become immobilized as we slowly become extinct."

Isla agreed, and within moments were on our way back to Zxentrux.

Chapter XV
SALVATION

Once we disembarked on Zxentrux, we returned to the boardroom and Isla's tutorial resumed. She said what we saw was proof that it was the responsibility of the inhabitants of any planet to be the custodians of nature and leaders of all living things.

She spoke with clarity and eloquence, "It is our duty to take care of all living things for the benefit of everyone, not just for the benefit of the elite. We learned that lesson the hard way and we want to share our mistakes and our corrective actions with you. We would like the two of you to take what you have learned here and somehow get the people on Earth to listen so you can avoid the mistakes we made on Zxentrux. It is not yet too late for Earth, but if you do not move quickly, it will be."

I carefully chose my words as I responded, "Isla, we are a determined and innovative population back on Earth and when it comes to solving a problem we do eventually rise to the challenge. We stumble along the road to success, but we do get there."

"You may not have enough time left to stumble," she said. "It is sheer luck that brought you here. We have tried on occasion to alert the planet Earth of their destructive path but the message has not been received. We watched mankind evolve from the early caveman days to now. We contacted your ancient civilizations but they either could not comprehend our intentions or they were unwilling to listen and so we agreed not to interfere with your planet."

The day was filled with one revelation after another. It was like Isla was a never-ending informercial about Zxentrux and climate change. By this time, I did not think there was anything that she could say that would surprise me, but she managed to do just that. Her next words finally put everything into context and I finally understood what brought us here.

She said, "We left instructions during your Roman period that would provide access to us when your modern civilization was ready to comprehend our messages. Unfortunately, due to the destruction of wars and the mere passage of time, our instructions became incomprehensible. The builders of the Pantheon somehow discovered our codes and incorporated them into their building. They had no idea what the markings meant but they preserved them, nonetheless. It was your curiosity that brought us to this moment."

I looked proudly at Clare and said, "I was the one that got obsessed with the markings, but Clare was the one that discovered the secret code purely by accident."

"Don't we make a good team?" Clare asked in a joking manner.

When I asked Isla where we go from here, she said she would like us to be her guests for dinner at her home. She felt that she had saturated us with enough information and that it would be wise to continue our conversation the following day.

She continued, "Your ride will take you to your room where you will find another wardrobe. Take a brief time to relax and when the two of you are ready, simply let the front desk know and your ride will pick you up and deliver you to my home."

It all sounded so normal and so much like our lives on Earth. On the ride back to the room, Clare and I tried to make sense of everything. We both agreed that of all the revelations that we had seen and heard that day, the one that was most unforgettable was witnessing the destruction of the old planet. What also resonated with us was that Isla felt that we faced the same destiny on Earth if we did not act quickly to reverse the effects of climate change. She did not refer to what destroyed her original planet as climate change, but the description of what killed it was exactly that. We felt that it was incumbent on the two of us to somehow alert our planet of skeptics and conspiracy theorists and make them believe us before it was too late. It would be a massive undertaking to re-educate our planet. Would we have to go to the extreme edge of disaster before we realize that we can only survive through cooperation? Even if we could get through to our fellow human beings, our technology could never catch up with that of Zxentrux in the time that we have left to reverse the destructive path that we are on.

Then an even more frightening thought came to me. What if we cannot reverse the effects of climate change and we become a mere chapter in the history of the universe.

I spoke to Clare tentatively, "I don't think we will see an honest effort to reverse climate change unless we experience true loss or at least visualize it. We are a civilization motivated by a fear of failure. I'm afraid that if we continue to let things slide at home, it will be too late to make corrections."

We were both caught up in the enormity of the moment and sat silently holding one another's hand until we finally arrived at our hotel. In our room we found a new wardrobe of semi formal evening wear. Clare reached into the fridge and poured us a couple of drinks. We walked over to the large window and looked out as darkness set in and the two moons appeared on the horizon. We were carrying a great weight on our shoulders, and it all seemed so overwhelming. Our lives were going so well back at home. These issues were reported in the media but they did not seem to be having much of an impact on us personally, so they did not seem like something that needed our imminent attention. We realized that we had become complacent, and we were living with a false sense of security that there was no need to panic. The hurricanes, floods, drought, and wildfires were events that happened elsewhere to other people. We were safe and secure and isolated from these disasters and we watched them from an arm's length thinking it could not happen to us.

The pursuit of wealth and success made us oblivious to the damage we were inflicting on ourselves and others. We were blind to impending disaster because we had been living in our own smug, isolated little world. Politics and a distrust of science had created a world of skeptics and climate deniers. We had been living with the mentality that if it is not happening in our back yard, it does not concern us. We looked at disasters unfolding in different regions of the world as something to deal with in the future rather than something that needed immediate action.

"You know Clare, I think we have always assumed that science and technology will get us through the climate change crisis. This past day has made me realize that science and technology alone cannot fix this. We need to act. I think a good analogy of what is going on with climate change is the Titanic. There are warnings that we are heading for disaster but we have chosen to ignore them. Sometimes it is just easier to live with our heads buried in the sand. As we are having a fun time eating, dancing, and singing, we are ignoring the fact that we are heading to our demise. Just as the watchmen on the Titanic warned of the approaching iceberg, our scientists are warning us of impending disaster. And just like the Titanic there will be no turning around. The song and dance will stop, and panic will take over. Our civilization will disappear. The majority of the population will perish," I mused out loud.

After moments of what I assumed was reflection, Clare attempted to break the intensity of the moment with a bit of sarcastic humor and said, "That was pretty deep, Jim."

She made me laugh and steered me to a lighter mood. I was now ready for our big night out at Isla's house. We dressed in our finest Zx-entrux couture, called for a transport, and by the time we reached the lobby, our vehicle had arrived. Our ride took us to the outer edges of the metropolis past neighborhoods now shrouded in darkness. Children were returning home after a day of play as adults were heading home after a day of work. Robotic street cleaners were systematically moving up and down the streets. Refuse and recycling vehicles were collecting the day's offerings. We passed playgrounds and parks and then all signs of urban life suddenly disappeared and we were moving past wide-open fields and rolling countryside, off in the distance with the occasional wildlife probing for their next meal. Every so often we could see lit windows peeking out through stands of trees and tall grasses. We approached a hillside with a large, light filled window stretching along the one side. Below was a pond of water reflecting the shimmering moon. The vehicle pulled up to a covered section of the building and stopped in front of a large glass entrance. We had reached our destination.

Isla and a gentleman stood outside awaiting our arrival. We exited the vehicle and greeted one another warmly. Isla introduced her partner, Sim. After exchanging pleasantries and handshakes, we moved inside to a gallery-like space filled with artwork and sculpture.

Clare was the first to speak.

"This is a beautiful place. I love this room," she said in awe.

"We have spent a lifetime together collecting these works. These pieces were created by artists on our original planet," Sim replied proudly.

As we were admiring the artwork, a robot arrived with a champagne type substance. We each grabbed a glass and Sim made a toast to us and we thanked them for inviting us to their home. We strolled through the room into an area that housed a large table, chairs and glass cases filled with sparkling artifacts. Once we seated ourselves, I started the conversation by asking Isla and Sim if they had always lived in this area.

Isla picked up the conversation by saying, "I was born and bred in this city. My mother and father are still alive and live in a nearby retirement community which addresses their specific needs. We were a family of average means. My father worked in construction and my mother was a teacher. I enrolled in university and studied science and environmental studies. It was there that I met Sim and we have spent our time together travelling around the planet studying and experimenting with ways to improve life here. After our graduation we got involved in council affairs while also establishing a bio business to help growers get higher yields from their crops. It was a very lucrative business. After fifteen transitions we sold our company and got fully immersed in council affairs. I started at the division level and after ten transitions, I became the lead council of our planet. Sim is a consultant to the local council on affairs dealing with environmental issues."

Clare asked if they have any children and Sim replied that they have one son who is currently studying away from home.

He continued the conversation and said, "I was born in another metropolis and grew up working for my father who was a grower. Eventually I moved here to study, I met Isla and the rest is history. I never looked back."

It was at this point that I joined in the conversation and said, "Clare and I also met in college. I studied project management and Clare studied economics. After graduating, we bounced around working for different companies in various parts of the country. Eventually we settled in South Carolina where I established a business and Clare became a compliance officer for a leading financial institution. We have one child. She is married now with a child of her own. We felt the world was overpopulated and did not want to be a part of the problem, so we did not have any more children."

"I completely understand," Sim responded. "Our ancestors suffered due to overpopulation on the old planet. Thankfully, we have learned our lesson here."

Isla abruptly changed the subject and said, "Enough small talk. It is time for dinner. You must be hungry. I have studied your cuisine and I have mixed your foods with our traditional fare for what I hope is a wonderful, pleasing dinner for all of us."

She said that she loved to cook. For her, it was a form of relaxation that took her mind off the everyday issues that they faced. Within minutes, as if on cue, two robots with trays appeared and set plates filled with food in front of us. While one or two of the food items were familiar, the others were unrecognizable.

"This looks delicious," Clare said politely.

Isla explained that their food is both naturally grown and engineered.

Clare took a tentative taste and exclaimed, "The taste is wonderful. I'm not sure what I am eating, but I love it. The flavor is so intense."

Throughout the meal, the robots methodically went about replenishing our drinks, and bringing out course after course of food.

I asked Isla how they dreamed up the concept of a house buried in a hill.

Sim took over the conversation and said, "Our civilization is built to be covered by natural soil and vegetation. We had this built after selling our business. We were fortunate that we did not reach the level of wealth where the wealth cap would be levied on us, so we were able to be extravagant in building our home."

I changed the subject and asked Isla about the robots. The robots had me intrigued and I could not resist asking about them. I was curious if they were an affordable addition to a household or if only the wealthier citizens were able to procure them.

She replied, "Not everyone has a robot, but obtainability is not necessarily determined by cost. Rather, it is more about practicality. Smaller, less wealthy families can retain them, but it depends on their priorities. Since we both work all day, virtually every day, we felt that it was a necessity for us. If one of us chose not to be employed, we would probably only need one robot to help out. They have become a part of everyday life for our citizens. There are different models that perform distinct functions for specific needs."

Next, I asked if the council has any top-secret programs that utilize advanced science and technology. I expected her to say no, but instead her answer surprised me.

"Yes, we do. They are on a strictly need to know basis for Lead Council knowledge only," she said and shut down the line of conversation as abruptly as it began.

After we finished our meal, we moved to a room facing out over the pond. The hilly countryside and fields were lit up by the two moons shining in the sky. It was a breathtaking view. When I told Isla how beautiful the area was, she said they chose this location specifically for the view.

When I asked about heating and cooling a home built into a mountain she said they use the earth as a source of heating and cooling through a geothermal system similar to what we would refer to as a heat pump on Earth. Various methods are used to power the pump. The most prevalent and most practical way to produce energy is through solar and wind methods. They also use electromagnetism. Battery storage plays a significant role as well. She said their technologies have devised ways to store energy without depleting valuable resources. All the knowledge they have gained over the previous transitions has been used to build an energy efficient planet.

It was getting late and we thanked Isla and Sim for a wonderful, informative evening. After a round of hugs, we bid them farewell, and headed back to the canopy where our ride awaited us. It still amazed me that no one needed to call for our ride. We arrived at our hotel exhausted from a long day, and after a quick night cap, we quickly slipped into bed and were asleep as soon as our heads hit the pillow.

The next morning, we awoke to what was supposed to be our final day on Zxentrux. We quickly got ourselves ready, grabbed breakfast and summoned our ride. We were curious about what this day's topic would be, and we were anxious to know whether this really would be our final day here. As much as the people on this planet were hospitable and friendly, there was always the possibility that this was a ruse. As fascinating as this planet was, we missed our home and our family and were anxious to get back to the life we knew. Activities that we had previously taken for granted, we now looked forward to. We could not wait for our routine morning jog and commute to work. We could not wait to see our daughter and grandson once again.

At the council building we made our way to the boardroom where we sat and waited for Isla to arrive. She quickly entered the room and took her seat. After exchanging our routine good mornings, she said they enjoyed our company last night.

"We loved it as well. You would make great neighbors," Clare said to her in her usual Clare-like way. "Any chance you would move to our planet? We could be best friends."

Isla thanked her for the invitation but said she had unfinished work to do on Zxentrux. She then said that the council had agreed to provide us with the engineering to complete a carbon capture structure for our atmosphere. She said they would also provide other methods of carbon reduction and power generation. As I thanked her, she handed me a thumb drive saying that they no longer use them on Zxentrux, but since we still use them on Earth, all the information we needed was on the memory drive that she handed me. She said it held all the information that our engineers and scientists require to clean our atmosphere within ten transitions.

Next, she said the words that I had been hoping to hear.

She said, "Now we must get you back to your planet. You will need the clothes that you came in. We will return you to the place where we found you and we will ensure that the transition to Earth takes place when there is no one around. There is only one condition. We will have to erase the memory of how you were able to connect with us. You will not get your codes back and copies of the codes will dissolve from all devices and surfaces that they appeared on. There will be no sign that they ever existed after you leave Zxentrux. This was a one-time event and your planet will not be able to reach us again until you have achieved the ability to reach Zxentrux through space travel. This may take hundreds of transitions. Your memories of everything else will remain intact. It will be up to you how much you share with your planet and how much you wish to divulge with those in charge. You may face strong political and scientific critics who will try to diminish your experiences. We wish only peace and good health to your population and to your planet. We will be watching for any progress made on Earth. It was my pleasure to meet you and I wish only the best to both of you."

I thanked Isla and asked her to pass our regards on to Sim.

"Please express our deepest gratitude to the council for this gift that is so desperately needed on Earth. We will miss your hospitality and your beautiful planet," I said with absolute sincerity.

Clare, once again on the brink of tears, added, "I am so sad that we may never meet again but we will cherish the time we spent with you. You have a beautiful planet and I hope one day we too will reap the rewards of a life filled with clean fresh air and water."

We had met them only a few days ago, but it felt like we were leaving lifelong friends. Isla led us to a room where our dark clothing was waiting for us. She then escorted us to the transporter room where our space craft awaited. Once the wall opened, we entered and waved goodbye to our new friends. The opening slowly shut and we looked out the window as the panoramic view lit up. The craft lifted off and we were thrust into space. The ride once again took us on a rare, once in a lifetime trip past constellations, galaxies, and planets. Eventually Earth came into view and we were hovering far above Rome. It looked so dark and desolate. Suddenly we dissolved and reappeared in a smaller craft that took us down to the Pantheon. We dissolved once again and were deposited in the exact spot that we left two days ago.

I looked at Clare and said, "Welcome to Rome. That was quite a trip."

It was quiet and dark as we moved to the alter and collected the bag we had left behind. Miraculously, it was still there. I mused that their security sweeps needed improvement. We dressed in our street clothes, hid ourselves under the alter and fell asleep. We awoke to sunlight beaming into the building through the large opening overhead. We could hear chatter and surmised that security must be in the building. The sound of the clicking and clanking of locks and latches filled the silence of the room. Finally we heard the large bronze doors open and the sound of tourists entering the building. Street sounds mingled with the excited voices. We were anxious to leave but knew that we had to be patient. It took about half an hour before we could move from our perch and safely blend in with the crowd. Slowly we worked our way through the throng of people marveling at artwork. We gradually made our way to the entrance, casually walked out the door, and once we had safely exited the building, we darted across the Piazza and down a narrow street back to our hotel.

In the safety of our room, we collapsed on the bed.

"Oh my god Clare, did that really happen? No one is going to believe this. I'm not sure if we should mention it to anyone. They will think we're insane," I said wearily.

Clare sat up and looked at me intently.

She said, "We have to pass this information on to someone who can put it into action. Somehow, we will have to convince them that we are not a couple of lunatics and this really did happen. The information on the memory stick could save our planet."

We agreed that we had to sit down and figure out to whom we should give this information. We knew that we could not take too long because time was running out for the planet. Every day that we hesitated, would be a day the planet moves closer to extinction. We grappled with how much we would tell our confidant about our alien abduction. Just saying those words among the two of us sounded crazy. If we were to say them to anyone else, they would have us committed. We were both tired and agreed that we needed to get back home first and worry about it later. Our return flight was two days away, but we were ready to go home the next day. We were officially vacationed out. Clare rescheduled our return flight for the following afternoon. We were unable to rest and decompress, so we started packing, and checking our phones and laptop for any evidence of the markings. Just like Isla said, there was no trace that they ever existed. I do not know how they did it, but somehow, they did.

We later went for a walk among the ancient ruins and read the plaques that told various historical tales. It was a warm afternoon and the streets were full of tourists. We stopped at the Trevi Fountain and could feel the cool mist of the spray. We took the obligatory tourist selfie with the fountain in the background. Our hunger overcame us, and we went to a trattoria and had a light lunch to tide us over until supper.

The food on Zxentrux was good, but there was nothing like cheese, salami, and olives. Afterwards, we made our way back to the hotel and sipped on wine in the lounge until dinner. Evening was upon us, and we decided to stay put and eat in the hotel dining room. After a course of spaghetti and fresh salad we took a final evening stroll through the city before returning to our room and falling into a fitful sleep.

Chapter XVI
HOME SWEET HOME

Despite an exceptionally long sleep, we both awoke exhausted the next morning. After showering and dressing we grabbed a quick breakfast, rolled our luggage to the valet, and handed him our ticket. Within minutes our car arrived and we were on our way to the airport. After dropping off the rental car we moved quickly to the airline desk to check our bags and get our boarding passes. Once we cleared all the required checks, we made our way to the gate. An hour passed and our flight was called. We took our business class seats and settled in for the long trip back to our corner of the world. At our home airport we cleared customs, retrieved our bags, and headed for the parking lot. After an uneventful flight, we were once again safely at home.

It felt so good to see our house, smell the familiar smells and know that our daughter and grandson were not far away. We could go for a morning jog, visit friends, and eat Clare's home cooking once again. Even the thought of going to work and the stress and tedium that were a part of it sounded enticing. It was comforting to see that everything was just like we left it a week ago. The only difference was that we were not the same people that left this house. We had an out of this world experience and we had no one except one another that we could share it with. At least, not just yet.

After we unpacked, Clare opened a bottle of wine and we sat on the couch as we routinely did, except this time, we both felt unsettled.

I looked at Clare and asked, "Where do we go from here?"

After a long pause, she replied, "The way I see it is that we have three options. One we go to the government and inform them. Two we go to an organization like the United Nations. Three we send an anonymous package to either one or to both."

While she spoke, I had a revelation and said, "There is one more option. We could release it to the press. That would create a shit storm, wouldn't it?"

Clare looked at me and said, "It does sound like a good option, but the talking heads would make us look like a couple of lunatics. We have to really think this through and consider all angles before we decide to give it to someone. If we give it to our own government, we will be under scrutiny until the day we die. Big brother will be watching. They may silence us and do nothing with the information."

We ultimately decided not to give the memory stick to our government because it was a global issue. We were concerned that the information could be used as leverage with other nations rather than shared for the common good of the planet. The United Nations seemed like our best option. Clare had contacts that might be able to help us maneuver our way through the organization and get it into the right hands. Next, we had to mutually decide how much of our experience we would share and who we could trust with the information. It had to be someone with enough confidence in our mental acumen to know that we were not lunatics and action would not have to be taken to protect us from ourselves.

We knew that until the experts reviewed the memory stick, our story would not be believed. We discussed whether we should get a scientist or an engineer on board before we go to the United Nations. If we could enlist a respected expert to review the material and convince them to be our spokesperson, it would give us more credibility.

We would not present as the crazy old couple from South Carolina with too much time on their hands. After more google searches than I could count, and an ongoing debate between the two of us, we decided on Stephen Harris, a world-renowned MIT professor known for his global revelations and predictions regarding space, time, and science. He would be a brilliant and credible advocate if we could only get him to meet with us. When he speaks, people listen. We decided to split things up. Clare would work the United Nations angle and I would contact Mr. Harris.

We spent the next few days cutting grass, pruning, gardening, and doing other routine household chores. The physical exertion helped us wind down, and once the chores were completed, we had time to take a lazy paddle along one of the winding rivers near our house. We spent time with our daughter and grandson.

On the weekend, we fired up the grill for burnt offerings with our longtime friends, Joe and Martha. Later we sat around a bonfire with them, roasted marshmallows, and reminisced. We talked about old times and decided that we should plan a trip with them sometime in the future. Our friend Jean would be the person to contact. She arranged great trips. She was a retired travel agent we met in Buffalo who had travelled the world and had made particularly good connections with operators in the world's most interesting locations. We appeared to be relaxed and at peace with the world as we socialized with our friends, but we were actually bursting on the inside, wanting to share our experience with them. We needed to talk about what happened, but we knew that it was better left unsaid, at least for now.

The evening quickly ended and the sense of well-being and normalcy followed us into the house. But once the kitchen was cleaned up, and we poured ourselves a glass of wine, the conversation inevitably switched from the exuberance of the evening to the wonderment of the previous week's adventures. We were overwhelmed with the acute sense of responsibility that had been thrust upon us. Saving the planet was up to the two of us and we knew that we would not be able to do that without coming across as a couple of old screwballs.

Chapter XVII
A NEW WEEK

Monday morning arrived and the rat race was about to begin. In a strange way I welcomed it. Catching up on the backlog of the previous week should take my mind off our Rome adventures. Sure enough as soon as I entered the office I was confronted with the issues of the day. Schedules were not being met and costs were running over budget. I maneuvered my way through meetings and phone calls and did not think about our dilemma until I took a break for lunch. While eating at my desk, I googled Stephan Harris' information and found his email address at MIT. I carefully wrote a message asking if he would be willing to meet to discuss a groundbreaking innovation that I believed had the potential to reverse global warming and save our planet. It was worded in such a way that it would catch his attention and not prompt him to delete it. Finally I needed a subject line that would entice him to open the email. I decided to go with *Stephan Harris is a fraud*. I hit the send button and off it went into cyber space. If I had any regrets, it was now too late. Hopefully, it would work and get his attention.

The rest of the day was spent battling the problems of the workplace and looking for solutions. It passed quickly and before I knew it I was on the road and home again. That evening we shared our results.

I told Clare about my e-mail. She was not impressed and made it clear that she did not think my subject line was clever. In fact, she told me that I might have blown it and the unopened email would be reported as spam. She said he might even see the email as a security threat. Once she was done expressing her frustration, or as some would say chewing me out, she told me that she had been successful in reaching her contact and he knew someone at the United Nations that might be receptive. The person her friend contacted was the head of the Science and Technology Commission and Claire hoped to hear from her in the next couple of days. She then sarcastically said that she hopes that I am as successful with Mr. Harris. She was usually quite supportive of me and rolled with the punches, but the previous week had a profound effect on her. She was feeling the urgency of our mission. My usually easy-going wife was missing in action.

The next day I arrived at work, and after a brief discussion with Mackenzie, I shut my office door, fired up my laptop, and eagerly waited to see if there had been a response to my email. I started thinking about how technology had changed us. When I was in university, I had to put a stamp on an envelope and wait days or weeks for a reply. Now I am impatiently sitting in front of a computer, frustrated with the minute that it was taking to boot up. The home screen suddenly appeared and I clicked on the email icon. There were twenty-five emails in my inbox. Five rows down I could see that Stephan Harris had responded and I quickly opened it to see what he had to say.

The first paragraph read, *Nice trick Jim. You got my attention. I took the liberty of researching you on the web and what I found made me consider your request seriously. Obviously, you are not a crackpot or a threat to my safety. My schedule is quite full but I will call you Friday at noon. We can talk and see if a meeting is warranted.*

This turned out much better than I expected. My phone number and company name that always appears on my email signature helped give me credibility and it gave him something to research me with. I immediately left Clare a voicemail and told her that she did not have to worry any more, my gambit was successful.

More meetings, reviews, phone calls and negotiations filled the afternoon hours, tempered by more cups of coffee. Before I knew it, my workday was done and I was eagerly heading home to show Clare his printed response. She was just as excited as I was and as we had been doing way too often these past few weeks, we opened a bottle of Prosecco to honor the moment. I made a mental note that we had been drinking more than we normally do, but I decided that I would worry about it later. This development was way too exciting not to celebrate.

That night I once again had one of those horrific, vivid dreams that lingered after I awoke. Even though I was holding myself together in my waking hours, whatever dread, fear, or stress that I was feeling seemed to be visiting me in my sleep. This dream started out with meeting Stephan Harris and sharing the data with him. He was fully committed to being our front man and would lead the show at the United Nations. All would go well until the equipment was built and launched. That was when things went off the rails. Once everything was in place, the aliens from Zxentrux commandeered it and turned it into a massive laser cannon. Helping us to save our planet had been a ruse. The mothership had taken over the cannon's control systems and it was aiming at high value targets. We were defenseless. Our planet was not equipped to fight this type of war. We had spent too much time fighting one another to develop equipment capable of fighting aliens. Buildings, bridges, and infrastructure were destroyed. Our planet was being annihilated. Rather than saving the planet, Clare and I had unintendedly brought about the destruction of Earth. We were now existing in a desolate wasteland. We had been duped. All the kindness and sharing of technology was a ploy to conquer our planet.

I awoke in a cold sweat. Clare was already awake. She said my thrashing and the unintelligible sounds coming from my mouth scared her. She thought I was in physical distress.

I told her about my dream and asked "What if this information we have is actually a Trojan Horse? What if they saw us as the perfect unwitting fools to get their plan in motion?"

She paused for a moment and then quietly said, "We have to go on faith. Do you really believe that after all we experienced those people would do something like that? We have to take them at face value. This is just your imagination running wild again."

I tried to get back to sleep, but it was impossible. It had never occurred to me that the people on Zxentrux were not sincere. Maybe they were evil and they were using us to destroy Earth. After that nightmare, work would be a welcome distraction.

The rest of the week was filled with the routine tedium of the workplace. When I was not on the job, I tried to fill the hours with chores and exercise to stave off the apprehension I felt regarding my impending conversation with Mr. Harris. I worried that he may not call and I worried about what he would say if he did call. Whichever way the conversation went, it would be a defining moment. It would dictate how we would move forward with the information we were given, and if we would move forward at all. I was keenly aware that our lives were now centered on the little memory stick in my pocket rather than our friends, family, and work. I knew that it was not healthy to be so obsessed with something but I still could not readjust my focus.

Friday finally arrived and my phone rang precisely at noon. Just as he had promised, Mr. Harris was on the other end of the line. After politely greeting one another, he cut to the chase and asked what I had to offer and how he could help me. He seemed very direct and actually, a bit intimidating. Nervously, I thanked him for taking time out of his busy day to talk to me.

I started by saying, "What I am about to tell you may come across as delusional. You may even hang up on me when I tell you what happened but please hear me out before you do that."

My story started with our visit to Zxentrux, how it happened, and about all the things we did and saw. What I could not tell him was how we actually got there because that had been erased from our memories. Finally, I told him that the good people of Zxentrux provided us with the technological information needed to build equipment that would save our planet from burning up. There was silence at the other end.

"Mr. Harris, are you still there?" I asked.

He slowly answered as if he was trying to process the information, "Yes, I am. I'm trying to digest what you said. If what you are saying is true this could accelerate our scientific study. Do you currently have possession of this information?"

When I told him that I do have it, he suggested that we meet the following day at his office at MIT to review it. I told him that I would be on the first flight to Boston. Once I had my flight scheduled, I would email my arrival time and he could let me know when he was available to meet. He agreed and gave me directions to his office. Before he hung up, he told me that I did not have to address him as Mr. Harris. If we were going to partner on this project, I should call him Steve. I was stunned. He seemed to be taking me seriously.

I booked the rest of the day off and headed home. The first thing I did was give Clare a call and share the good news. She was thrilled that it looked like someone may take us seriously. Once I arrived at home, I immediately went online and reserved a ticket to Boston with an open return. I emailed the flight information to Steve, and I packed an overnight bag just in case our meeting went beyond one day. Clare was not home yet, so I went outside and settled in with a beer and soaked up the warm sun.

My phone was sitting on the table within reach in case Steve or Clare needed to contact me. I started musing about how that one little device had incorporated so many other pieces of equipment. It was amazing that this pocket-sized gadget could be a camera, a radio, a compass, a flashlight, and a clock in addition to being a phone. Whoever would have thought this would be possible when I was growing up? It would have been something seen on a science fiction show. Technology had advanced at breakneck speed and it helped us live better, less cumbersome lives. It also gave us challenges that we are still trying to deal with.

It felt satisfying to know that I may be holding the key to save mankind so future generations can live happy and healthy lives. The information on the memory stick could give our planet breathing room so it could start to repair itself and lead us to a better future. I sat back, sipped my beer, and listened to Vivaldi. The collection called the Four Seasons took on new meaning as I thought about how this information could preserve our climate. Once Clare came home, I suggested that we go out for dinner but instead, we decided to stay at home and watch the stars before we went to bed.

The next day, I was showered, dressed and on the road to catch my 8:00 a.m. flight long before my 5:00 a.m. alarm was scheduled to go off. Once I landed in Boston, I hailed a cab, zipped through the streets, and crossed the bridge to Cambridge. The driver dropped me off at the Green Building, marked number fifty-four. I made my way to Steve's office. I took a deep breath and paused for a moment to steady my nerves and then knocked on the door.

A voice from inside said, "Come in."

It was then that I had my first face to face visual of the man that I hoped would take me seriously and help save the planet. He was a tall gentleman of similar age to me and was sporting a lab coat as you would expect a scientist to wear. We greeted one another and exchanged small talk about the flight before we got down to business.

With a tinge of cynicism, he said, "Tell me more about these little green men you met."

He smiled and we both laughed. I realized he was evaluating me. My guess was that he was intrigued by my story and wanted to believe that it actually happened, but at the same time, he was skeptical. I once again recounted my story but with more detail. While I spoke, he looked directly in my eyes. Maybe this was his method of truth detecting. Whatever it was, his mannerism was a bit unnerving. With every description of the various technology and devastation we witnessed; he would nod his head as if he believed the information I was giving him was factual. I started with the markings on the old home movies and went on to our adventures in Rome and even the break and enter at the Pantheon. When he interjected and asked if I had copies of the markings, I told him that all traces had been erased.

When I paused, he said, "Ok Jim, let's see what you have to show me."

I pulled the thumb drive out of my computer bag and handed it to Steve. He told me to insert it into my computer. He did not say so, but he still had concerns that this could be a scam and the flash drive was a virus. I know that I would have been skeptical if I was in his position. The folder opened up and revealed five files. He clicked on the first one that revealed engineering drawings resembling the large carbon capture structures that Clare and I saw on Zxentrux. Steve scrolled through the drawing zooming in and out to get a better look at the details. He closed the file and clicked on the next one. It was filled with line after line of words and calculations. He studied the information carefully before scrolling down. He continued his search, combing through each file. He eventually closed the last file and rubbed his chin before running his hands through his hair.

He turned to me and said, "Jim, this is going to have an enormous impact. This is absolutely earth shattering. It will be the biggest scientific breakthrough that this planet has ever experienced. It is phenomenal. I will need the top scientists here to go over this to verify its accuracy. Authentication could take quite a while. Are you willing to leave this here with me?"

I replied, "As long as you can assure me that it is kept in absolute secrecy. We have already decided that it should be presented to the United Nations to avoid political issues. We have a contact that can introduce it."

He told me that he fully understood my apprehension and assured me that this would not become the next Manhattan Project. He went on to say that he had two trusted scientists that could do the analysis and we should be able to move forward on this within a week, provided that the information is accurate and authentic. He said he would be thrilled to represent us at the United Nations if the information checked out.

His tone softened as he said, "This is urgently needed for our planet. I commend you and your wife for your bravery and for the substantial risk that you took to get to this point."

He asked for permission to make a copy of the thumb drive to share with his associates. I did not have an objection and he proceeded to plug it into his computer and duplicate it. I thought to myself that he must be starting to trust me now. If this was something nefarious, he would not copy it using his work computer. Apparently, I am the only idiot that does that sort of thing.

He placed the copy in his pocket and said, "This will never be out of my sight and I will make sure that it is not duplicated. It will only be utilized in my presence. My associates will work from my computer."

He proceeded to hang up his lab coat and invited me to join him for lunch. I eagerly agreed. He led me to his car, and while he drove through the bustling Boston streets, I was busy on my phone making a hotel reservation for the night and setting my flight time for the next day. He did not seem to mind. Before I knew it, we were walking the crowded streets to a restaurant called Sea Fare. We were promptly seated near a window and the conversation once again turned to the information that I had just presented him.

We spoke in hushed tones. When I asked him what his honest opinion was, he whispered, "If all this checks out, it will take a massive effort to pull it off. The fusion generators alone are a huge breakthrough. The engineering in those records is astonishing. It would have taken us at least another fifty years to reach that level of sophistication. It is truly a significant acceleration of the technology that we have."

He said he was excited to get started and would give the information to his colleagues tomorrow. They could immediately start reviewing and verifying the data. Once it was authenticated, he would present it to our United Nations representative. I told him how relieved I was to have his support.

We exchanged our life stories over lunch. I quickly gave him a rundown of my education, my family, and my occupation. He followed by telling me that his fascination with science started at an incredibly early age. He attended prestigious schools and has travelled the world in the name of scientific study. He never married but had been in various long-term relationships. His only constant life partner has been his studies and work has been his mistress. He said his career has been rewarding but like all scientists he is always searching for answers to questions that have not yet been asked. From our conversation it was clear that he was distressed by how the planet was suffering at the hands of mankind. He said science is a double-edged sword. It has positive life-giving aspects but in the wrong hands it has led us on a path of destructive behavior.

He seemed to have a strong distain for social media and the wild west of disinformation. People were losing faith in science because it had become politicized and compromised through self-serving persons. He said he understood that science is not always exact. Theories have to be assessed numerous times. Timelines are always being redefined and that becomes unacceptable to the general public that expects immediate answers. He believed that it was this that led to distrust.

He continued, "There have been bad outcomes because of science, but just like anything else in life we are learning more at a much faster pace. As you can see, we are now faced with reversing the toxins and the change in climate that science and technology have brought us."

I replied earnestly, "I hope you can lead the charge to bring us back from the brink and save our planet. I know that it will take years of work but based on your credentials and the conversation we just had; I have utmost confidence that you can make it happen. The sooner we get started the better. We don't have another planet to call home so we need to fix the one we are on."

After lunch, Steve dropped me off in front of the Hilton. We shook hands and parted ways. I checked in and headed to my room. It had been a long exhausting day and I had another early start tomorrow. I called the front desk and asked for a 9:00 a.m. wakeup call. I quickly unpacked and called Clare to fill her in on the meeting. She was happy that it went as well as we had hoped. She said she would let her contact at the United Nations know that there could be a potential meeting this weekend. I hung up the phone, turned on the television to try and relax, only to find that Star Wars was playing. It was not something that I could enjoy at this point, so I decided the time would be better spent trying to get some sleep. By the next evening, I would be home safe with Clare.

Mid-week I got the much-anticipated phone call from Steve. The information had been verified by his associates and he said it was spot on. He seemed eager to set up a meeting at the United Nations but I told him that I would have to get back to him because Clare was the one with the contact. Her friend had already alerted the woman who heads up the Science and Technology Commission. She said she would be ready when we are. It seemed like everything was in place for a potential meeting. After I hung up the phone, I immediately called Clare and let her know that things were a go on the Boston end. Thirty minutes later she called to say that the meeting would be Friday, at 1:00 p.m. at the United Nations in New York City. We had clearance to meet with Anna Martin. I called Steve with the details and he said it worked for him. We agreed to meet at noon just outside the United Nation's main entrance.

Friday morning Clare and I were on our two-and-a-half-hour flight to LaGuardia. By 11:45 a.m. we were standing in front of the building's entrance. Within minutes I saw Steve get out of a cab.

When I introduced him to Clare, he looked at her with that direct gaze of his and said, "It is a pleasure to meet you. Your husband has told me wonderful things about you."

Clare reciprocated and said, "With all due respect, I don't think anything could top your accomplishments. I am honored to collaborate with you."

We moved on to the business we came to discuss. We decided that Clare and I would start by giving Anna background information about our experience and I would then turn the floor over to Steve. Without him, we would not sound credible. He would fill her in on his research and the viability of the memory stick. We walked towards the entrance. Once inside we provided the security personnel with our names and who we were there to meet. He made a phone call and ushered us into the elevator. By the time it stopped on the seventh floor I could feel my nervous tension elevating. By the way Clare squeezed my hand, I knew she was feeling the same way. In contrast, Steve looked cool and collected, like it was just another day on the job. We found our way to Anna's office and within five minutes she appeared and welcomed us. After introductions, she led us inside and closed the door.

She addressed Steve with reverence, "Mr. Harris, I am very honored to meet with you. I have read so much about your research. This must be particularly important for you to get involved. When Clare contacted me and told me you were part of the delegation I was immediately intrigued and wanted to meet as soon as possible."

Steve responded by saying that he has a great deal of respect for the work that the United Nations does. He said that trying to get representatives from various countries with divergent views to come to consensus must be much like herding cats. Anna laughed at the analogy. She said the work was daunting and frustrating at times but in the end, it was rewarding.

She quickly changed the subject and addressed the matter at hand.

She said matter-of-factly, "Clare tells me you have discoveries that will save us from self-destruction."

At this point, I spoke up and asked if I could fill her in on what brought us here. She agreed, and once again I went through the entire scenario starting with the old home movie and ending with the abduction by friendly aliens that wanted to help us. It sounded like a fantastical story but it was real. She sat back in her chair and was speechless. She was trying to process the story that I had just laid out for her.

Anna finally spoke, "You are kidding, right? You want me to convince our global citizens that aliens exist. There are nations represented here that refuse to acknowledge that climate change is real. I am getting heartburn just thinking about it. I can hear their response. If they do believe us, they will insist that we are being invaded and this is actually a trap. I just don't know what to say."

Steve jumped in at this point and took the lead in the conversation. He told her the material that he and his colleagues analyzed was accurate and would advance our technology forty to fifty years. He described in detail how it would work and what it would accomplish.

She was obviously overwhelmed and said, "That's remarkable Steve, but I have to think about how we can share this with the world. I will need all of your input. Jim, I will arrange for you to sit with one of my administrators so we can document your story. It will have to be written as an informative piece that is not meant to frighten. We do not want to panic the world. Steve, I will need you to help me produce a simple presentation to illustrate what these technologies will do for mankind and our planet."

Anna looked at her calendar and asked if next Tuesday would work for us. She said one of her assistants that is very adept at this sort of thing will be back in New York City on Monday. She would know how to navigate through this with the least amount of collateral damage. Steve and I both quickly agreed to return. Anna closed the meeting by thanking all of us for coming to New York City on such short notice and said that she looked forward to seeing us again the following week.

Back at home, Clare and I spent the weekend reading, sailing, and visiting our neighbors. After getting home from work on Monday, I packed for my return trip to the United Nations. On Tuesday morning I was sitting in seat 18D once again heading to New York City and to what I surmised could be a new chapter in the history of the world. At the United Nations I once again met Steve and Anna. Anna summoned her two assistants, Lacey, and Donna to her office. Donna was assigned to me and Lacey was assigned to Steve. They ushered us into separate rooms to start the documentation process. I introduced myself and asked Donna about herself. If we were going to work together, I needed to know who I was working with.

She spoke without hesitation, "I was born in San Francisco. My parents were computer programmers. I majored in English literature in college and worked for the local newspaper for about five years before applying for this job. Now tell me your story."

Once again I repeated my story as Donna set up her computer and started to create a file. She wanted to document the story starting with the old home movies and ending with the abduction to Zxentrux and the return trip to Rome on a spaceship. It must have sounded crazy to her, but if it did, there was nothing in her affect that gave it away. She just typed and asked for clarification when she felt I needed to expand on an aspect of the story.

After two hours, I was all talked out and the only response I got from Donna was, "Fascinating."

She went on to say that she has interviewed countless people in the course of her job and has listened to interesting and sometimes frightening stories, but she has never documented an account like mine. She politely thanked me for my time and said she would polish my story so it could be easily understood. It would then be translated to several different languages. She said it would take time to complete the transcript, but once she was done, she would courier a copy to me for my official approval. She did not want to risk sending it electronically.

I headed back to Anna's office where Steve and Anna were waiting. Anna was the first to speak. She said that she had arranged for a council meeting to take place in a week. We were invited to attend, myself as a witness and Steve as the expert. She thanked us for trusting her enough to share the information with her. With that, Steve and I left her office and headed over to our hotel.

After calling Clare to fill her in on what had transpired, I met Steve in the lounge for a drink and we decided to go to Armando's, an Italian eatery for dinner. The restaurant was infamous for its gangster ties in the early days. It gained notoriety when Mafia godfathers were assassinated there. We hailed a cab and we were quickly dropped off in front of the restaurant. Just as we were about to enter the building, sirens interrupted the sounds of the city. Suddenly a black Lincoln shot past us with police cars in hot pursuit followed by two yellow taxi cabs with flashing blue lights. Within seconds the chase faded away down the street.

Steve looked at me and said, "Welcome to New York City."

I replied jokingly, "I wonder if the people in the Lincoln had reservations here. If they did, maybe there is a table open for us."

We continued to lightheartedly banter back and forth. The successful morning had put us in a jovial mood. We were surprised to see that taxi cabs were used in police pursuits. We imagined sitting in the back of a cab when all of a sudden, the blue lights start flashing and you are holding on for dear life. If the passengers were unscathed in a possible shootout, we wondered what the bill would be for the extra distance travelled. We were laughing like two old friends by the time we entered the restaurant. As predicted, a table was available and we were immediately seated and served. Later, we decided to catch a burlesque show where the fan dancers and comedians entertained us until the lights were dimmed and it was time to leave. It was a relaxing end to a stressful day. The anxiety I felt earlier had melted away with the mirth and camaraderie we experienced that evening. I had a new friend who would have my back when I needed it.

The next day we shared a cab to the airport and after going through the usual security checks, we shook hands and went our separate ways. Despite the successful day I had in New York City, it felt good to be home once again. I spent the next day catching up on work. Two days later a package containing the transcript of the meeting at the United Nations arrived at home. After carefully reading the material, I was impressed with what a wonderful job Donna did transcribing my story. It was beautifully written and easy to understand. After I finished reading it, I sent her an e-mail telling her it was perfect and that she could proceed. I then emailed Steve to let him know that the eagle had successfully landed.

Within days, I received a formal invitation from the United Nations to attend the presentation along with Steve and Clare. The notice listed all the participants, what council chamber the meeting would be in, and where to pick up our passes. The enclosed list of world-renowned delegates from the political and technical world was intimidating. My heart was racing and my blood pressure was rising. It was getting real and soon it would be front page news. The moment of reckoning had arrived and I felt like a ridiculously small fish in an exceptionally large pond.

Tuesday arrived too quickly. Clare and I were once again walking into the grand council chambers with Steve and Anna. It was precisely

1:00 p.m. We arrived early to rehearse the presentation we were about to give. Anna and her assistants were prepared and ready to go but we were not as confident. After direction from Anna regarding timing issues, Donna turned on the large screen and quickly ran through the slides. She gave each of us a copy of the story line and an agenda. We went to our assigned seats and tried to stay calm while we waited. At 1:30 p.m. people started drifting into the room. I watched as they took their seats behind their country nameplates. By the 2:00 p.m. deadline, the room was full and the chatter was deafening. Anna stood up behind the podium and tapped the microphone.

She started with the customary, "Good afternoon."

After welcoming everyone, she delivered an introduction saying that today they would be privy to a historical event that could change the world and save mankind. Ten minutes into her speech, she finally asked everyone to refer to the handouts that were in front of them. She explained that outlined in the pages before them was the extraordinary chain of events that brought everyone together. She then asked Clare and I to stand up and she introduced us to the audience, lauding us for our bravery and willingness to share our discovery. Next, she introduced Steve who was given a round of applause. Anna described his input and his commitment to the work ahead. She then proceeded with her presentation on the giant screen. As images of one technological advancement after another flashed across the screen, sounds of astonishment could be heard. The once quiet chamber was now abuzz with discussions taking place while the slideshow continued. When the presentation finished, Anna spoke frankly to the audience. She said that to implement this would require a massive cooperative effort by every nation. The world would have to mobilize and bring together all the top scientists and engineers to tackle this global project. It would take years to achieve these goals and redirect the trajectory of the world, but it was necessary and the sacrifice would be worth it.

A question period followed the presentation. Each representative was given a chance to speak. While there were delegates that were visibly joyful and appreciative; others were inquisitive. Who would lead the effort? How would the responsibilities be divvied up? What is the timeline? There were also individuals that expressed skepticism and were not fully convinced. They were concerned that this may be a trap to invade and conquer Earth. Anna answered each question intelligently and with eloquence. She then appointed a committee of delegates to oversee the operation and set a 10:00 a.m. meeting with Steve and myself for the following day. We were to review our strategy and then world leaders would be contacted via the Secretary-General. The meeting adjourned and we followed Anna out of the chamber.

"You know we are going to have rock star status in the papers. Be prepared for what happens next," she whispered.

Anna was right. Our lives were turned upside down. We could not go anywhere without having news and camera crews following our every move. The story was splashed on every television screen and streaming service. We were getting calls from networks that wanted us to appear on their talk shows. We were booked solid for weeks travelling around the country and around the world. The President of the United States invited us for dinner at the White House. World leaders were inviting us to meet with them. We were enjoying our newfound fame and connections.

We attended a dinner at the Italian Prime Minister's home. We were excited that the Pope was expected to be at this gathering. After a lavish dinner, The Roman and Vatican Police entered the room and surrounded the two of us. We were shocked. The Prime Minister gave us a stern look, produced a document, and then read out the charges against us.

"You have been charged with unauthorized entry of The Pantheon and using religious artifacts for personal gain. These are serious offences and are punishable by honorary citizenship and a complimentary accommodation anywhere in Italy," he said in a deadly serious manner.

Everyone in the room burst into laughter. After processing what had just happened, we were able to relax and be a part of the levity. Each police officer approached us and shook our hands before leaving.

I turned to the Prime Minister and said, "Thank you for your hospitality and thank you for not throwing us in jail."

Everyone laughed.

"My pleasure. Your story has enticed scores of tourists to visit Rome. They all want to be in a small way connected to your discovery," he said.

The activities and appearances were never ending and exhausting but we reveled in the attention and accolades. It felt good to be globally acknowledged for something that was going to benefit mankind. We were no longer just an anonymous, aging couple from South Carolina, valued and loved by their family, friends and coworkers but invisible to everyone else. We now had a legacy. We always made sure to acknowledge the people of Zxentrux and their generous contribution to help save our planet from certain doom. I would look up to the sky during my interviews and think of Isla and tell her that if you can hear me on Zxentrux, we owe this all to you. We knew that we could never repay them for what they had given us but I hoped that generations to come would someday be able to share the rejuvenation of life on Earth with them.

One evening after I had thanked Zxentrux in an interview, Clare and I were sitting outside listening to crickets and frogs and looking at the constellations when what appeared to be a spaceship swiftly approached and hovered maybe one hundred feet above us. It shined a light down onto us and a hologram of Isla appeared. We stood up and gazed at the silhouette in amazement. We could hear Isla's familiar voice speaking to us.

"May our worlds one day meet in friendship. You will always be in our hearts and minds," she said as she stretched her arms out as if to hug us.

The hologram quickly dissolved; the light went out and the spaceship quickly disappeared leaving the two of us in tears. Clare and I sniffled as we hugged one another.

Clare was the first to speak, "I think we did okay Jim."

"Yes, we did," I replied.

Isla had just confirmed that the people we met on Zxentrux were authentic and that they were not using us for underhanded reasons. We had found a devoted friend in her and the people of her planet. She taught us not to fear others that may be different from ourselves and even in this fragmented world of division and misinformation, sometimes we just need to trust and have faith in one another. We just needed to accept and respect the differences amongst us.

Clare and I have often discussed why I was so obsessed with the drawings on my father's old movie reel. Honestly, I do not know what possessed me. There has not been a day that I have not thought about my father since his passing many years ago. He was a brave, unassuming man who came to this country with nothing and built a home and raised a loving family. He left this world with the legacy of being a good hardworking man, a good father, and a good husband. I saw him as a hero and maybe somewhere inside of me I wanted his legacy to reach beyond his family. Maybe I wanted the markings to have significance so he would be revered throughout the world. Clare thinks my dogged persistence was me wanting to honor my father. She said what I do not realize is that I honor him every day by being the person that I am.

She may be right, but there was something else going on with me. Our lives had become too predictable. We were empty nesters established in our careers and financially secure. We had been married for the majority of our lives and could anticipate what the other would say before a word was even uttered. Every day was usually a good day but it was a repeat of the previous day. We would get up, jog, go to work, come home, and go to sleep. I loved my life and realized how fortunate we were, but maybe we needed something to knock us out of our mundane existence. We took for granted the comfortable trappings of our secure world and had lost our sense of adventure.

When we started on our journey, we never expected it to end with aliens and being responsible for saving the world from extinction. Now that we have a couple of break and enters under our belts, have visited an alien planet and have been cited for bravery throughout the world,

I appreciate the quiet predictability of our lives. Maybe it took a whirlwind journey through the galaxies to be grateful for what we have.

Today, Clare and I still do our morning jog, go to work at our respective jobs, and watch the stars at night. What we do disagree about is how the events transpired. We were both there, we both experienced the same events and yet we remember them differently. We have lively discussions about what really happened and it keeps our relationship spirited and interesting. What we do agree about is that sometimes what you are missing in life is right in front of you and where you are meant to be is exactly where you are. And for me that is with Clare, our daughter, and our grandson in South Carolina. They are my true legacy.

Chapter XVIII
SUMMARY

We are approaching a tipping point on Earth and we do not have a planet like Zxentrux waiting for us to inhabit it. Drastic measures are needed. We cannot continue to be wasteful. Converting resources to currency has created a global crisis. Environmental degradation is saddling us with astronomical costs in health care and disaster relief. These costs not added to the products we consume, via an environmental fee that in turn contributes to the research and development of CO_2 reduction technologies. Unfortunately, this is not enough. It is time for us to pay the actual cost rather than the cheapest price. Industry that helped create the problem must contribute to the clean-up and consumers will have to pay more. Profits and dividends will suffer. The wealthy will need to refocus.

Waste and overabundance can only be minimized by conserving resources. Our capitalist society needs some fine tuning. Do we have a choice and do we have the will to do what needs to be done? Will it create political chaos? Will it create more poverty and less equality? Do we even care? These are questions that we must face and issues that we struggle with.

We can ignore the problem but our lives will change. We place trust in our elected leaders to make decisions in our best interests. Sadly, most of these decisions deal only with a short-term fix. The long game is not getting the attention it needs. The older population is banking on younger leaders to fix the problem while the young are pointing fingers at those who created this mess. Will the next generation be capable of making the sacrifices necessary or will they take the most effortless way out and continue on this destructive path?

We need resources with minimal environmental impact. Reducing consumption of inexpensive and disposable goods is needed to maintain an environmentally sustainable world. We need an innovative approach to capitalism. World leadership and coordination is necessary to encourage renewable industries and technologies. As populations continue to grow, we will need to raise the cost of nonrenewable commodities and reduce or subsidize the cost of renewable resources to make them affordable. We need an aggressive global shift away from our current economic philosophy towards one with an environmental priority that includes monitoring and enforcement. Financing massive carbon extraction projects and the reduction of methane will also help offset the environmental impact. Our stock exchanges must require businesses to have an environmental component to their business model such as contributing to an environmental cause.

We can suffer minor pain now or severe pain and expensive costs later. If we do not act, consequences such as floods, devastating storms, deadly heat, food deficiencies, drought, civil unrest, market and economy crashes leading to potential war between the haves and have nots could be in our future. Until we can successfully turn things around, the earth will struggle to sustain life as we know it. These dire circumstances might sound like doomsday fiction because we currently live in a time of plenty. But much like a cancer, the planet's demise is spreading undetected and will reach a point of no return unless it is treated in time.

We have one chance to turn things around. Everyone will have to play a small part in transforming and ultimately saving the planet. The wealthy need to play a bigger role in the solution. As individuals, we can do our part by reducing our dependency on consumer goods and services that are non-essential. We can limit the amount of individual use products we buy and insist on biodegradable packaging. This will add to the cost but it will send a message to industry.

Should our current civilization disappear, Mother Earth will eventually heal herself and grow. As long as the sun keeps shining it will go on with or without us creating a whole new cycle of life. Millions of years from now, inhabitants will be digging up our remains trying to determine what led to our extinction. As a global society we need to strengthen our sense of humanity and feel empathy for one another and our planet. We need to appreciate our fresh air, our forests, the splendor of nature and the majesty of wild animals rather than take it for granted.

We need to repair what is broken. We have the technology to make changes happen but do we as a global community have the will. Progress has outpaced technology. Maybe it is time to slow things down and allow technology to catch up.

Fortunately, we as a global community are implementing measures to make meaningful changes. People around the world are paying attention and taking individual steps. There are focused improvements in prevention, reduction, and extraction of toxic pollutants. There are alternative sources of renewable energy such as wind, solar and tidal power. There are improved efficiencies in energy storage, motion technology, agriculture, recycling, waste reduction, and clean-up efforts. Artificial Intelligence, ecological, biological, scientific, and medical discoveries are happening at a rapid pace. The study of nature is teaching us how to live as part of the ecological framework and work with the Earth to clean and sustain it. We have stepped up the filtration and composting of plastics and waste products. We just need to scale it up exponentially.

Most innovations are carbon producers during the initial stages of the development and manufacturing process. The equation includes the premise that the carbon used to create these innovations would be offset at some future time making them carbon neutral. Does the eventual offset justify the means? Not all ventures will be successful. There will be failures. But we have to start somewhere in order to transition to a carbon reduced environment.

Large charitable tax-exempt organizations could be tasked with finding solutions at a more rapid pace. We could consolidate all the environmental innovations that are being created into a central global organization or data bank. We could divert funds away from non-essentials and support environmental nonprofits on a much larger scale. Every human being leaves a carbon footprint. It accumulates from the moment you are born. Developed societies leave a larger carbon footprint and yet it is the poorer countries that suffer the most from global warming. They have a smaller footprint, but they are impacted the most.

More transparent monitoring is needed so we can see if and how our efforts are making a difference. Similar to weather and finance reporting we need environmental graphics on a regular basis. How much do a million trees planted in South America help to reduce carbon? Has cleaning the North Sea of garbage contributed to cleaner fish? A global analysis and reporting system is needed to track our progress. We need to collaborate with one another and know what is happening around our globe.

Are we going to let our civilization die off? Is this the final destiny that we are willing to accept? When we harm nature, nature fights back to survive. The inhabitants of Earth will lose the battle unless we learn to live in harmony with our planet. We need a workable agreement not to destroy the ecological balance that keeps us alive.

Our biggest challenge and number one priority remains the accumulation of carbon dioxide (CO_2) and methane in the atmosphere also known as greenhouse gasses (GHG). Carbon dioxide has accumulated over the centuries and is now having detrimental effects on our climate and our lives. It is caused by the conversion of fossil fuels to energy. As the earth's temperature rises, vast frozen portions of the planet are thawing and releasing more stored methane and carbon dioxide. Peat beds store tons of carbon. As they are drained or dried, they can no longer absorb it and start to release carbon. Trees and plants capture and retain carbon but release it all to the atmosphere when they burn. Grasslands are more efficient at capturing carbon by driving it back into the earth through their roots. Composting also helps to retain carbon in the soil.

Carbon in the atmosphere is similar to a blanket that never comes off, keeping us warm in the winter but stifling us in the summer. Each year we keep adding another layer. This accelerates the melting of ice caps and raising sea levels and temperatures, adding more carbon to the atmosphere while killing marine life. A cooler planet helps oceans, forests, and grasslands to capture carbon more effectively. All the carbon dioxide that has been generated over the centuries does not dissolve or escape our atmosphere. It accumulates and even if we stopped producing carbon dioxide today it would only slightly reverse the effects we currently experience.

Methane takes about twelve years to dissipate. It is released by the earth when we drill. It is emitted by animal husbandry. It also escapes every time we cook with natural gas not to mention the use of decorative gas features. These are the things we know about. There are probably many more emitters in countries that we do not have access to.

We can alter these emissions and reduce carbon and methane in our atmosphere through more efficient processes and through changing the diets of man and animal. It is a huge ask but it is also a huge cost if we do not act. Trees and oceans cannot clean the air in time to save mankind from itself. It cannot be done without help from us and especially if we are burning, cutting, or bulldozing them down. We need to prevent carbon dioxide from entering the atmosphere. We need to capture it and find ways to make it inert. Hopefully, we can reverse the downward trend before it is too late. The doomsday clock is ticking and we are seconds away from extinction. Business, Science and Technology got us into this mess. It will have to get us out of it. It is time for action.

Survival is our only priority at this juncture.

Nothing else will matter if we don't address climate change.
We have two options.
To do something about it or slowly watch humanity go extinct.

About the Author

Robert lives with his wife Donna and their cat Clipper in South Carolina, the Palmetto state. He studied Project Management at Toronto Metropolitan University, Canada and had a long career in heavy industrial construction that took him around the world. Consulting, coaching, and mentoring occupy his time now. This is his second book. The first published work *When We Were Young* is a book which chronicles the life and times of a young man and a woman who established a family and network of immigrants after living worlds apart conquering their individual struggles for survival during a destructive war starting a new life in the land of opportunity.

9 798822 943513